CW01652736

THE GRINGO TREES

To John Dunlop,
My best wishes to a true patriot.
My best,
Bill Doswell
Oct. '92

The Gringo Trees

J. William Doswell

Taranis Books
Glasgow 1991

typeset by Media Bridge

design by Alan Mason

published by Taranis Books*

printed in Gt. Britain by Bell & Bain Glasgow

*Taranis Books is an imprint of

MEDIA BRIDGE

For J. N. Reilly

PROLOGUE

Lupe sat on the ridge overlooking the Pacific, body bent forward, arms hugging her drawn-up legs. Emilita had left as soon as the grave was filled; gone shuffling stiff-legged down the hill, whining about what would become of her now. Lupe was glad the old woman had gone. Her grief was private.

The ocean was slate gray in the late afternoon. The water undulated in long rhythmic swells, movement set into motion thousands of miles away now completing its journey on the flat beaches of El Salvador. Wind traced fitful patterns on the surface out beyond where the waves broke in the shallows. But on the ridge it was still and hot and on Lupe's blouse sweat stains fanned out from beneath her arms.

Clouds were building off shore, straining warmth from the faint sun. As a child the clouds had fascinated her, huge, towering clusters. Later, she knew they'd turn orange at the edges, fading to pink as the sun fell below the horizon. Lupe looked at the clouds and knew it would not rain, that the clouds would break up and scatter in the early darkness and finally race across the moon when the wind shifted as night wore on. By dawn, it would be calm again. She could not explain how she knew this; but she knew it as surely as she knew that married couples who heard gekko lizards in the roof thatch on their wedding night would have good luck.

Lupe looked up the beach and then turned and looked south. The view was the same, palms in uniform rows, ocean and sand beaches. It came to her, her entire life - all that had mattered - had taken place within sight of where she sat. She had never before considered her immediate surroundings as a perimeter of her life's activities; more precisely, the core.

She shifted, straightening her skirt as she stretched her legs full length. A gull flew over and she watched it riding the air currents, its cry quickly fading, lost.

"Gone," Lupe whispered, "So quickly gone."

Within six weeks, the substance of her life had been destroyed; all she considered meaningful and dear wiped out as completely as she could erase a mark in the sand. Why had God directed his fury at her? Had life not been hard enough?

Below her a breeze flirted with the tops of the gringo trees. Their swaying fronds stirred memories and she lay back, eyes closed, and remembered.

The gringo trees. How long had it been -- six, seven years?

"Who planted the trees so straight, Lupe?"

"Gringos, Tomas."

"What are gringos?" He was a skinny little boy and his shiny black hair hung over his ears and grew down his neck. His deep brown eyes were serious as he looked up at Lupe, waiting for her to answer.

Lupe's face split into a smile. She hugged the boy to her. It was warm on the ridge where she and Tomas sat, waiting for Emilita to catch up.

"Gringos are what we call white people." She rubbed her arm to show him. "Here, where we're tan, they're white."

"All over?"

"Yes."

"Why?" he asked.
"Who knows?"
"Do I know any gringos?"
"I don't think so. They're gone now."

Tomas looked down the ridge at the rows of trees that stretched along the beach like formations of soldiers standing at attention. "I'm going to call them gringo trees," he said solemnly. They'd been gringo trees ever since.

Before Tomas named them gringo trees, they were palms. When Lupe was a child, families gathered there for picnics. Gringos operated the farms then. On Saturday afternoons after work, everyone from the village crossed the ridge and met under the trees. Children swam or walked the beach while mothers gossiped and kept an eye on them. The men fished, or sat in the shade, talking and drinking cerveza. There was no hint of war. Food was plentiful, people were content. Life was good.

Years later, in the evenings, she and Juan would slip away from the village and meet among the trees. It was their place to be alone. All young people need and find such a place.

It was beneath the palms that she had gotten pregnant, twelve years ago come July. Juan was not to blame, she was as eager as he.

Emelita did not see it that way. She told her friends, "That boy took advantage of Lupe. And now, when it is time for her to birth and she needs a husband around, he's run off to sea."

"I have to go," Juan explained to Lupe. "There's no work here, no way I can take care of you. But I'll be back. I promise you."

They had carved their names on a tree within two hundred yards of where she now lay. It was their pledge - his promise to return, her's to wait for him. She had not looked for the mark in years but she thought of it now.

How many days had she come to the ridge and searched the ocean for incoming ships, praying that one was bringing Juan back to her? How many times had she looked out over the gringo trees and cried, frightened and despondent? It was a bitter, lonely time and Lupe had needed him desperately. Finally, she did what she had to. There was no other way to feed Tomas and Emilita and keep them together as a family.

In twelve years Juan had come back nine times. He always brought money and presents. But, he always left again. Then, four months ago he had returned, this time for good. It seemed to Lupe that God had finally heard her prayers.

ONE

"Aiee, that's a hard pull. The last few yards seem steeper than last time." Juan crested the hill and mopped at his face with his shirt sleeve. He was sweating and his breath came in gasps. "I think the rain washed the steps away."

"It hasn't rained. It's too much beer. That," Tomas said, grinning, "and you are getting old."

"You wait until I get my breath and I'll show you how old I am. I'll teach you to pay me some respect," Juan said, swatting at the boy with his palm frond hat.

Tomas jumped away, laughing, and easily avoided the blow. "You know I'm kidding." He stretched his thin arms above his head. "What a day. Feel the breeze. I don't care whether we catch any fish."

"If you don't catch any, your belly will care tonight," Juan said, straightening. He looked out over the ocean two hundred yards away. The ridge on which they stood sloped down through scrubby bushes, the dirt chalky white. "Without the sea, we'd starve. It's always been that way."

The Pacific was a palette of blues in the morning sun. Far out where the freighters steamed hull down against the horizon, it was dark, deep and mysterious. Closer, where dolphin hunted just beneath the surface and smaller fish jumped to escape, the water was slate blue. Closer still, where the bottom sloped up gradually to the shore, it was turquoise, a warm blue-green through which the white sand of the bottom looked milky as waves flattened and disturbed the silt in a constantly resettling motion. In its wake, scurrying sand crabs dug furiously, small piles of wet sand testimony to their industry.

"This is my favourite place," Tomas said softly. He was tall for eleven and his ribs could be counted through the golden skin of his chest. He crossed his arms above his head and rested them on his shiny black hair. "It's the only thing I really like here. I don't mind the walk."

"You're right," Juan said. "It's worth the walk even though the last few steps are straight up." He took off his shirt, sliding the unbuttoned sleeves over his hands. His chest was nearly hairless and slick with sweat. Pulling his hat low over his eyes, he peered straight out to sea. Where the sky met water a smudge of smoke trailed off to the south, nearly lost in the heat haze.

"A ship's heading north," he said.

"Where?" Tomas asked.

"There," Juan pointed. "Way out. See the smoke at eleven o'clock, low on the horizon."

"I see it," Tomas said. "Wonder where it's headed."

"I don't know. Mexico, maybe. The United States. Who knows? She's too far out to put in up the coast. If she was going to come in at La Liberdad she'd be in closer."

"Wonder where she's coming from?" Tomas spoke the words dreamily. "What's she carrying?"

"Probably Chile or Peru or somewhere else in South America. Or, she could have come through the canal in Panama."

"I'm going to sail on one like her some day," Tomas said.

"You've got a few years to go," Juan answered.

"I'm nearly twelve," Tomas countered.

"You've still got, maybe, five years," Juan said, swatting at a fly that worried around his head. "Times have changed.

You got to be older now."

"How old were you when you left?" Tomas asked.

"The first time? I don't know, fourteen maybe. Shipped out on a coaster hauling logs from Honduras to the States." He pushed his hat back on his head and his voice turned sour. "I miss it like hell, but my sailing days are over. That's a fact, like it or not."

He held up his left arm and looked at it before letting it drop to his side. From the wrist down the hand had been mangled. Only the thumb was distinguishable. Where the fingers had been, the flesh had been folded over and stitched together into a shapeless form that resembled the end of an oar. Juan lifted his useless hand again and looked at it with disgust.

"No place for a one-handed man at sea," he said. "And I'm fast finding out there isn't much of anything for a one-handed man to do ashore."

"How did it happen?" Tomas asked. He looked at the withered hand and couldn't conceal the revulsion it evoked.

"I bet I've told you a hundred times since I came back four months ago," Juan said peevishly. "What the hell's wrong with you, don't you listen? If it wasn't for my damn hand we wouldn't have anything to talk about."

"I know but I want to hear again. Come on, Juan, tell me."

"Have you forgotten?"

"You know I haven't. I'm just interested. Now, tell me."

Juan shook his head resignedly. "For the last time, Okay? We'd put into San Diego. Tied up at the pier and were unloading. I was helping at number three hatch amidship. One of the cables parted close to the winch and somehow got caught around my hand. Sliced the fingers off before I knew what was happening." He held his hand out before him and stuck it close to Tomas' face.

"Doesn't look like a hand, does it?"

Tomas shook his head. "No."

"Funny, on rainy days I can still feel the fingers. I know they aren't there but they feel like they're there." Juan clenched the muscles of his arm and the stump turned from pink to white. "Now, you satisfied?"

Tomas looked at the hand. The skin was lighter than the skin on Juan's arm and, at the nub where it was stretched tight, it glistened, waxy and pale. He thought it ugly. Taking his eyes off it, he turned to Juan and said, "Yes. I'm satisfied. I'm sorry it happened though. We might have sailed together one day."

"You really set on going to sea?" Juan asked.

"Yes," Tomas said. "I want to leave here."

"You got to have hair on your prick before you go to sea," Juan said.

Tomas looked out over the sea. He was embarrassed. He raised his eyes to look at Juan and they showed his anger.

"Does hair on your prick make you a better sailor?"

The answer prompted a flicker of a smile from Juan. "No, of course not," he said. He thumped Tomas on the back with his good hand. "But, you just finished telling me this was your favourite place. Why do you want to leave?"

"There's nothing to do here," Tomas said. "I don't want to take care of Angel the rest of my life. She's a good cow but what kind of job is that, tending to a cow? Or sweeping up the cantina. Nothing ever happens here. I want to make some money and see the world."

"Can't blame you for that," Juan said. "There's never been much in El Salvador that I can remember. Now, there's even less. Hell yes, boy, go to sea. Get the hell out of here."

"I'm going to," Tomas said.

"But now, let's go swimming, eh?" Juan led them down the hill toward the ocean. When they hit level ground they entered rows of palms planted in long symmetrical rows.

"Shade feels good," Juan said. He leaned against a tree and fanned himself with his hat.

"How'd they get them so straight?" Tomas asked.

Juan shrugged. "I don't know. They were here when I was a kid."

"The gringo trees."

"What?"

"That's what I call 'em - - gringo trees."

"You're crazy, kid, know that?"

"Why?" Tomas asked. "Lupe said gringos from the fruit company planted them. Why not call 'em gringo trees?"

"Call 'em what you like." Juan laughed. "You're something else."

"Tell me about them."

Juan stopped fanning. "What the hell's wrong with you, boy? We come here three, four times a week and you always ask the same questions."

"I know. But, it's the only time I have to talk about other things. Emilita is always ordering me around. Wash your face, move the cow, milk the cow, put the cow up. Go to town for a bucket of water. I get damn tired of it." He picked up a rock and threw it at a tree trunk. "You're the only one I have to talk to about things that really matter." He scuffed another rock free from the dirt and threw it as hard as he could.

"How about your friends?"

"I hate them," Tomas said. "They tease me about Lupe."

"What about Lupe?" Juan said.

"They say she's a whore," Tomas said.

Juan stopped walking. His face tightened. When he spoke his voice sounded flat and hard. "What do you think?" he asked.

"She's a whore," Tomas said. "Everybody knows it. Guillermo told me she does it with anybody for money."

Juan studied the boy's face. It was a mixture of hurt and defiance. They were still under the palms facing each other. Silently, Juan turned away from Tomas and began to walk toward the ocean.

"You know it too, Juan. Lupe is a *puta*," Tomas said, walking after him.

Juan stopped and grabbed Tomas roughly with his good hand. "Whoring is a job. Like fishing or butchering pigs. And in that way Lupe's a whore. But, Lupe's also a friend, the best one you got. She's a whore because there's no other way for her to make a living. She has to do it. But she doesn't have to be your friend, she's your friend because she loves you."

They had to come out from the shade of the trees and the sand was hot on their feet. "Understand that?"

Tomas shook his head. "I guess."

"Now get your ass in the water before you burn your feet off." Juan began to run toward the ocean. "Don't you ever be ashamed of her," he called over his shoulder.

They reached the sea's edge and sunk their hot feet into the sand. Juan took off his pants and stood naked. His belly was flat and he scratched it and then his chest. He tossed the shirt and pants onto the sand beyond the waterline and sailed his hat at the pile. "You ever think where you'd be without Lupe caring for you? She does the best she can."

Tomas stepped out of his shorts and threw them up on the beach. He sank his feet back into the sand and looked down into the shallow water. He did not answer Juan.

Juan leaned over and scooped a handful of water and emptied it over Tomas' head. "One last thing. Don't let on to Lupe that you know she's a whore. And, don't say anything that will hurt her. If you do, and I hear of it, I will beat the hell out of you, one hand or not. You understand?"

"Why're you so mad all of a sudden? I haven't done anything," Tomas said. "But I understand what you're saying. I don't plan to say anything."

"You damn well better understand it," Juan said, staring at him until Tomas turned his head. "Now let's go swimming."

He ran through the shallows to the deeper water, his brown body glistening in the spray he kicked up.

Tomas chased after him, diving into the water when it reached his waist. He came up, spit a mouthful of water skyward and laughed happily. He began to swim, finally turning onto his back and floating. The serious talk was forgotten.

They had caught four mackerel. The fish were laid in the cast net, gills gulping, flopping in the upper reaches of the tide. They were not big fish, running about a pound each, but it would make a good dinner.

Juan and Tomas sprawled naked in the sand, only their

feet in the water as it washed onto the beach. It hadn't taken them long to catch the fish. They worked the small net well together.

"Juan?"

"Yeah."

"I'm glad you're back." Tomas paused. "I mean I'm sorry about your hand, I really am, but I like having you around."

"Yeah, me too."

"Remember when we caught the big turtle?" Tomas asked.

"Yeah. How long's that been - - three, four years? It'd be fun to catch another," Juan said. He was on his back, eyes closed.

"Maybe we will."

"Maybe. But not now. It's not the season for them to come ashore," Juan said.

"We could make another basin out of the shell," Tomas said. He rested on his elbows. The heat felt good on his body. "Then Lupe and Emilita could use the old one and we could have the new one to ourselves."

"Maybe it will happen," Juan said. He yawned, and stood. He pushed his hair back with his good hand and walked back out into the surf and sank into it to wash off. Looking at the sun, he said, "We've got to go."

"Do we have to go?"

"Yes, it's after two. By the time we get back and clean the fish and you do your jobs it'll be time for dinner."

"Okay ," Tomas said.

Juan came out of the water and bent over and touched his toes. "It feels good to stretch. Everything feels good here. I'm like you, Tomas. I like this place, too."

Tomas was pleased. It made him feel good that Juan agreed with him. He stood up and put his pants on and picked the fish up.

"You better think twice about being a sailor," Juan said. "It gets cold up north. That's why gringos pay a lot of money to come down here in the winter. You can't believe how cold it gets."

"I don't care, I want to see the world like you," Tomas

said. "I don't want to milk Angel the rest of my life. I'm sick of that cow." He flung the fish over his shoulder. They felt cool on his back.

Juan put his shirt and pants on and pulled the hat down low to shade his eyes. "It's hard to figure. If I hadn't gone to sea, I'd still have my hand. Maybe I should have stayed here all along."

"You'd have always been thinking about the sea, about what you were missing," Tomas said.

"Maybe."

"At least you did something nobody else around here ever did."

"Yep, I did what I wanted."

"That's important," Tomas said.

"Yeah? What'd it get me? A useless hand and no job."

Juan took the fish from Tomas. "C'mon, kid, let's go."

TWO

They had finished eating and sat at the table while dusk swept the sun's last rays away. In the faint light that remained, the adults were quiet, content. Music from a radio faded in and out.

"Sounds like the batteries are going," Juan said. "About time, I guess. They've lasted four months of constant playing."

"When the kerosene truck goes to La Liberdad, I'll ask Pepe to pick some up," Lupe said. "I've really enjoyed it."

"Should have bought some extras in the States," Juan said. "Slipped my mind you can't buy anything in San Sebastian."

Through the door that opened into the backyard Tomas watched a chicken, head jerking, approach and peer in. He kicked at it and it retreated, ruffling its feathers, then began pecking at the bare ground.

"I'm going out for a while," he announced.

Emilita stopped picking her teeth. Her face was crisscrossed with wrinkles and the skin beneath her neck hung in loose folds that shook when she moved her head. Normally, her hair, near full grey, was pulled straight back from her forehead and gathered by a shell concha at the back of her neck. But she had washed it in the afternoon and tonight it hung loose and full.

"The water bucket full?" she asked.

"Filled it this afternoon," Tomas answered.

"All right, go. But be back by ten o'clock, you hear?"

"Yeah," Tomas answered and was gone.

"He runs free," she complained.

Lupe stretched and began to collect fishbones on one plate. Her eyes were dark brown, nearly black like her hair. She winked at Juan and smiled, her teeth white in her full mouth. "He's a boy," she said. "Boys that age need a little room."

"Ah," Emilita said, "he is still too young. He shouldn't be roaming around after dark."

Lupe stood and gathered up the plates. She took them to a table that stood in a corner and began to wash them in a pan. After washing them, she waved them in the air and leaned them against the wall to dry. The water, where she shook them, fell to the earth floor, the damp spots quickly absorbed in the dirt.

Juan cleared the rest of the table and set the dishes by the wash pan. Standing behind Lupe, he put his arms around her and pulled her to him. She paused from the washing and leaned back into him. She was nearly his height and their bodies fit like spoons.

"Lupe, Lupe, I've known you - what, twenty years - and you still arouse me. I swear you get prettier."

Lupe's eyes closed and she swayed from side to side. She smiled and lay her head against his shoulder. "You're either blind or crazy, but I love you for saying it."

Juan hugged her tighter. "I mean it," he said.

Eyes still closed, she turned and put her arms around his neck, pulling his mouth to hers. She kissed him, lips parted in lazy lust, then pushed him away and put her hands alongside his cheeks. "Juan, you're sweet. But, I'm beginning to fall apart. My breasts are starting to droop. Look how my ass sags. And, my belly has a roll of fat all the way across."

He caressed her left breast with his good hand. The nipple began to swell and harden. "No difference," he said.

"Stop this. Have you no shame?" Emilita said, pushing herself up from the table. She held the loose dress out from her and swept tortilla crumbs into it.

Juan laughed. "Patience, Emilita, you're next."

Emilita smiled and shook the crumbs out the back door. She moved with a shuffle, legs stiff from the waist. The trunk of her body had thickened with age but her arms were thin. "I'm going to get some air, it's too hot in here," she said, going out the door.

Lupe pulled away from Juan. "Got to get these dishes done, get ready for business."

"I hate it," Juan spoke angrily. "You whoring for a living."

"Think I like it?" Lupe said bitterly. "I hate it too. But, you were gone to sea and there weren't any jobs. It was do it or starve. There was nothing else for me to do."

"I know," Juan said resignedly, "but it stinks. How do you think it makes me feel - knowing the woman you love is the town whore?"

"How do I think it makes you feel! How do you think it makes me feel?" Lupe said caustically. "I *am* the town whore."

"I'm sorry, Lupe." Juan kissed the back of her neck and went back to the table and sat down. "It's just ... this damn place makes me sick. No jobs, nothing to do. Tomas was talking about it today. He wants to go to sea."

"I wish him luck," Lupe said. She wrung the dish cloth out and hung it over the dishes. Taking the dish pan to the door, she threw the water out. Chickens made a frantic dash for it.

"He's a good kid," Juan said. "Smart, too. I enjoy fooling around with him, for the first time really getting to know him."

"He's crazy about you. He's so glad you're back. Besides Pepe, he doesn't know anyone who's been past La Liberdad. You're his hero."

"Helluva hero. One hundred per cent failure."

"Juan!"

"It's a fact. I'm living off you and Emilita. Shouldn't have come back."

"Come on now, that's no way to talk."

"It's true, though." Juan sighed and stood up. "I hope Tomas does go to sea. Nothing here for him. Nothing here for anybody." He took Lupe's hand. "Let's sit outside for a while."

"All right, for a few minutes. Then I have to get ready," she said.

They sat on a wooden bench, backs against the hut's wall. It was dark among the trees but light still hung in the sky.

"Let's move away from here, Lupe."

She sat up, startled. "Where would we go? What would we use for money?"

"I don't know. But I'll never find a job here. I'll wind up being a bum. And you ... you whoring - - it's a helluva life."

"Agreed. But, we have a roof over our heads and food to eat," she said.

"Maybe I could get a job in La Liberdad." Juan spoke louder, his voice raised in enthusiasm.

Emilita appeared in the doorway. "Did you call?" she asked.

"No. I didn't call," Juan said.

"Somebody said something," Emilita persisted.

"We were just talking," Juan said. "To each other."

"Secrets, eh? Hiding something from me." The old woman's voice was bitter.

Juan sprang up. "No, damn it, no secrets. I just suggested we might consider moving from this damn place to La Liberdad."

"Shit," Emilita spat the word out as if she tasted it. They heard her shuffling off within the house.

"Damn old meddler, always sticking her nose in. No privacy at all," Juan said.

Lupe took his hand. "Don't blame Emilita. Think about it. What would we do in La Liberdad? There aren't any jobs. We don't know anyone. We'd wind up like we are now. Me, whoring, you frustrated and mad. And, Tomas, learning a lot of bad things." She put an arm around his shoulders. "Be happy with what we've got. When I get old and the customers stop coming, we'll look back on these times and wish we still had them."

She leaned over and kissed him. "Now, I must light the lamp. They won't show up if they don't see a light."

"I hope not a damn person comes," Juan said bitterly, stalking off into the shadows.

"No customers, no cerveza and tortillas, it's that simple," Lupe said, going inside. In a moment she reappeared with a lamp, a pan of water and a towel. She walked across a cleared space in front of the house to a thatched hut at the edge of a grove of trees fifty feet away. It was smaller than the hut she'd left, just one room, but that was all the space she needed. She lit the lamp, trimmed the wick and put down the globe. Crossing herself, she sat down to wait.

THREE

Tomas checked the rope that held the cow to the tree. There would be pure hell to pay if she got loose and they had to look for her in the morning. The last time it had happened was not his fault. Antonio and Jaime had turned her loose as a joke. But Emilita had blamed him and had raised whelps on his back with the cow rope.

He pulled at the rope and smiled as he remembered his revenge. He had peed in the old woman's bed. Her howls of rage softened the memories of the blows on his back.

The cow eyed him distrustfully as he pulled on the rope. She backed off and the rope stretched taut and held. Her tail swished back and forth and her eyes were wide as they rolled nervously.

Tomas picked up a rock and threw it at her. It struck her flanks and she reared against the rope and trotted off a few feet. "One night, Angel, I am going to turn you loose for good. Then Emilita can hunt you down while I am off sailing. How do you like that, you dumb, old cow?" He darted at her, as if to run her down, and she spooked and lumbered away from him. He laughed and left her, disappearing into the trees.

He headed for the field behind the cantina. It was the favourite meeting place of the boys of the village; they met there every night. Tomas went to the field knowing he would have to pay the price. He was the smallest and always got teased. But he was lonesome for company of those near his age, so he went and took his lumps.

They had built a fire and were talking about the soldiers when he approached. They were stretched out in the grass, relaxed. Except for a wave from Enrique, nobody paid him any attention.

"I sneaked up and saw them put their tents up," Guillermo bragged. "There must be fifty." Guillermo was the oldest and the largest. He already had hair on his prick. When they went swimming he always paraded around so they could see it.

"Why are they here?" Pepe asked. "Why do we need soldiers?" His father owned the cantina and they tolerated him for that reason only. He bought their favour by stealing bottles of beer which they drank and then flopped about in exaggerated stages of drunkeness.

"To guard the coast," Guillermo said. "They think campesinos are smuggling guns in. I heard them say nobody from the village can go to the beach anymore."

"But we need to fish," Tomas exclaimed. "We've got to have fish to live." The words came forth without thought, a declaration of fact.

The boys looked at him as impassively as they would a gekko lizard. Six pairs of eyes stared at Tomas from around the circle of firelight. Guillermo sat up and pulled a smouldering stick from the fire. He threw the blackened stick at Tomas. Tomas dodged and it hit behind him in the grass, sending up a shower of sparks.

"Tell them, Tomas," Guillermo said scornfully. "I'm sure the soldiers will listen to you. After all, you're the son of a *puta*." They all laughed.

"I am not," Tomas said. He sprang up, close to tears. "You're a liar."

Guillermo came around the fire and the other boys stood up to form a loose circle. "Everybody knows Lupe's a whore. And everybody knows she's your mother," Guillermo said, pushing Tomas in the chest.

"It's a lie," Tomas yelled, falling back a step from the push.

"Then why do you live with her and the old woman and the one-hand man?" Guillermo asked. He grinned and looked at the others and they grinned back.

Tomas looked around the circle. It seemed to close tighter around him. "I have always lived there," he said finally. He knew no other answer.

"Know how Juan's hand got that way?" Guillermo stood over Tomas, smirking.

"An accident, unloading a boat," Tomas answered.

"Nah, nah. God gave it to him as punishment for jacking off so much."

"Then you ought to have one, too," Tomas said angrily. "Maybe two."

"Smart guy, eh?" Guillermo pushed him again and he fell back into Jorge. "Why are you shoving me?" Jorge asked, and pushed him back toward Guillermo. All the boys joined in then, pushing Tomas back and forth until he lost his balance and fell to the ground, kicking and crying.

Grabbing a leg, Guillermo dragged him away from the fire. "Hey, here's a new game," he said. "Get his other leg, let's play *puta* ball."

They pulled Tomas around the fire, yelling and poking at him. At first Tomas struggled to defend himself. It was no use, he couldn't get loose. He finally gave up and went limp.

Tiring, Guillermo threw Tomas' leg away from him and flopped down on the grass, heaving from exertion. "You should be glad the soldiers are here," he gasped. He lay back on the ground, arms flung wide. "Business will be good for your whore-mother. Everybody knows soldiers only drink and screw."

"She'll make a lot of money," Jorge said.

"They'll keep her busy," Pepe said. "My father says

business will be good. He's ordering extra beer. When soldiers get drunk they want to screw. Your mother and my father will get rich."

Tomas turned over and got to his knees. His shirt was dirty and torn and his back hurt from being dragged. He stood up and blew his nose in his hands. He trembled in anger and frustration. He had stopped crying but his cheeks were streaked where tears had cut through the dust.

Guillermo looked up at him from where he sprawled in the grass. "How'd you like the ride on your back, Tomas? Now you know how it feels to Lupe." He laughed and the others joined in at the joke.

"I hate all of you," Tomas screamed. "I hope you all die." He jumped past the fire and ran into the darkness.

The boys' laughter followed him for a long time.

FOUR

Sergeant Emilio Sanchez walked into the cantina and stopped just inside the door. It was a small room with whitewashed walls and dirt floor. The only light came from three kerosene lamps spaced along the bar. Five round, wooden tables, each with four wooden chairs, were arranged in the area across from the bar. Sanchez looked around in the dim light and felt at home. It was a familiar sight. He had spent seventeen years in the army of El Salvador and had seen many cantinas like this.

Pulling out a chair, the sergeant sat down heavily and took off his cap. He wiped sweat from inside the brim with three blunt fingers and tossed the cap onto the table.

He had a broad face, more Slavic than Spanish. His high cheek bones were more common to the Indians that lived in the area near Nicaragua. His eyes were black, and the only thing about him that seemed to move quickly. He was short and stocky with powerful arms and shoulders. Years of drinking had thickened his belly and he grunted as he leaned over and unlaced his boots. Freeing his feet, Sanchez ran them back and forth in the dirt and slapped the table with the flat of his hand. "Cerveza," he called out to the bartender. He slouched in the chair and stretched his legs full length before him.

Pepe's father hurried to fill the order. He opened a bottle, wiped a glass clean on his apron and walked quickly to the sergeant's table. "Here you are Sergeant," he said pleasantly.

Sanchez ignored the glass and turned the bottle up. Taking several large swallows, he exhaled noisily and set the bottle down. "Damn, that's good, nothing like a cool beer," he said. He leaned back in the chair and silently considered Pepe's father who still stood holding the glass. Beer glistened on the sergeant's full lips and foam lingered on his moustache. He drained the remainder of the beer and held the empty bottle out to Pepe's father. "Another," he said. "Can't you see it's empty?"

Pepe's father returned to the bar and the sergeant belched and looked around the room. Several men stood at the bar and a few of the tables were occupied. Nobody looked at the sergeant and talk had dried up. The only sound was Pepe's father opening a beer.

Sanchez smiled. They were afraid of him. That's the way he wanted it. He was an uncomplicated man. He did not want to be more than he was. Twice he had rejected Lieutenant's bars. He didn't want to be an officer. To accept officer rank was to accept authority and regulation. As sergeant he *was* authority, absolute. He ran his platoon of forty eight men as he wanted and as long as assignments were carried out, officers left him alone.

It was a good life, being in charge. He had come a long way from the orphanage at San Vincente. He didn't allow any interference with his system. If anybody bucked him he beat them senseless, punished them severely and extracted *mordita* - a bite - from their pay. He intended to stay in charge.

Pepe's father returned with the beer and the sergeant took it without acknowledgement. Pepe's father continued to stand by the table.

"Well," Sanchez growled, "Why're you standing there?"

"We're glad you and the other soldiers are here," Pepe's

father said.

Sanchez took a long pull of beer and set the bottle down. Sweat beaded on his forehead and he leaned over and shook his head like a dog. He cupped his face in both hands and drew them back over his thick, black hair. Wiping his hands on his pants, he leaned back and picked up the beer.

"So you are glad we are here," he said, pointing the bottle at Pepe's father and wiggling it back and forth. "I'll tell you why you're glad. You're thinking in that rat's brain of your's that you'll sell a lot of beer and make lots of money off us soldiers." He drank again and wiped his mouth with the back of his hand.

"Well, let me set you straight. If I find that you raise the price and try to cheat my men, I will run a bayonet up your ass and cook you over a slow fire."

"I am only trying to be friendly," Pepe's father said uncertainly. He shifted nervously from foot to foot. "I don't cheat anybody."

"I know, I know," the sergeant said. "The best way to be friendly is to keep the beer cold and the price low. Now, get me another, eh?"

The men at the bar had left, edging out quietly while Sanchez and Pepe's father were talking. The tables emptied now. Sanchez watched them go, eyeing the women but saying nothing. Only Pepe's father and Sanchez remained in the cantina.

For an hour the only sound was Sanchez calling for another beer and Pepe's father serving him. When he had drunk nine beers, the sergeant crossed to the bar in his bare feet. Pepe's father eyed him warily; he did not appear drunk but one could never tell.

"I hear there's a whore in this town," Sanchez said. He eased himself onto a bar stool.

"There is," Pepe's father said. He was relieved the sergeant did not ask for another beer.

"Do you know her?"

"Of course. It is a small town. Everyone knows her," Pepe's father said.

"I mean know her - - as a man knows a woman," Sanchez said, swaying on the stool. He put a foot on the floor to steady himself and leaned towards Pepe's father. "You know what I mean," he said. His thick lips parted and he ran his tongue over them and they glistened in the lamplight.

Pepe's father busied himself putting empty bottles into crates. He stacked the crates until they were three high along the side of the wall. He did not answer.

Sanchez hammered at the bar with his hand. "Answer me, I asked you a question."

Pepe's father turned from the crates. He was breathing heavily from the work. He flipped sweat from his forehead before he spoke. "Yes, I know her. Since she was a child. And, when my wife was carrying our children, I visited her. But, not when my wife was well."

"And ...?" Sanchez drew the question out.

"She is all right."

"All right. That all? All right."

"She is a *puta*," Pepe's father said. "She does what she is supposed to do."

Sanchez laughed and stood up. "Well, barman, I'm going to visit her now. I'll see for myself if she's all right."

He walked to the table where his boots and cap were. He put the cap on his head. Tying the laces of his boots together, he hung them around his neck and started to leave.

"It is hot, give me a beer for the road," he said.

Reaching the door, he took a drink and stopped. "What is this whore's name?" he asked.

"Lupe."

"Lupe, eh?"

"Yes."

Sanchez took another drink. "Good night, bartender," he said, and went out the door.

He did not pay for the beers he had drunk and Pepe's father did not mention it to him. He blew out the lamps and said a short prayer for Lupe.

FIVE

It was eleven o'clock and Lupe walked outside the small building where she accepted customers and looked up at the sky. The moon was three quarters full and there were no clouds to hide the stars. They spread across the heavens, a bright gathering of dancing lights.

She looked across the clearing at the house. All of the lights were out; the others had probably gone to bed. She sat down on the bench. It had been a pretty good night. There had been two customers, both regulars. They transacted their business comfortably, as old friends, and went along. They would be back the next week and the week after. Lupe wished she had thirty like them.

Years before she had started equating money she earned with articles she could purchase. Tonight she figured she had earned flour for a week, some snuff for Emilita and a half dozen beers. If she could average two customers a night, she could feed the family and put a little in the can buried in the dirt beneath the chest in the bedroom. It was a small village and she did not often average two customers a night.

She stretched her legs out and considered the news about the soldiers. Business should pick up, she thought. Perhaps she would need another can beneath the chest.

Once she had been lucky, lucky in a way that comes to a person seldom in a lifetime. A young American had spent a week with them. He talked to Emilita and to Tomas and to her; long conversations that rambled on about religion, economics, education, everything that made up their life. Sometimes he took pictures, often without telling them, before they had time to pose.

It had been during one of the times when Juan was at sea, a vacant period in her life that Lupe measured with her heart. The American had come to the village and had stayed with them, paying for room and board. Often he sat in the dark with Lupe and talked with her when she was between customers.

He had put it all down in a notebook, answers to the questions he had asked. He talked of politics, of the church, of how life compared now with what it was like in Emilita's childhood when the padrones had owned the land. He was a nice man and they had talked openly of their disappointments and dreams.

The strange thing was that he never became a customer. This bothered Lupe and she resented it. Was she not good enough for this gringo?

"He thinks I'm not good enough for him," she told Emilita.

"Perhaps, but I don't think that is it, Lupe. I think he is different," the old woman said.

"You mean he likes men?"

"No," Emilita said. "I don't think sex is important to him." She shook her head knowingly. "I do not trust him. He has strange interests, maybe he practices voodoo."

Lupe was not certain. She looked at her body and felt her breasts. She was firm and full, a real woman. She washed and combed her hair, painted her fingernails and put a bougainvillea bloom behind her ear. By God, she would show this gringo what a woman she was.

But he did not yield to her and she began to keep a closer eye on Tomas. She finally accepted that he had no sexual interest in her or Tomas and came to like him as a friend. Emilita remained suspicious and said he was there to put a spell on them.

When he left the American had given her two U.S. $100 bills. It was more money than she had ever seen, and she had ridden the kerosene truck into La Liberdad to exchange it for Salvadorean money. It had supplemented her earnings for nearly four years.

Emilita persisted in thinking that he had bought their souls with such a vast amount of money. For a year she lit candles and prayed a special prayer to ward off spells.

Lupe prayed also, that he would come again. A long time later she received a letter from him. In it was a newspaper article with pictures of each of them. Emilita would not touch the paper, insisting it was cursed. Even though Lupe could not read the article, which was printed in English, she kept it stored in the drawer of the chest.

She had given up hope that there would be more customers and was ready to turn out the lantern when she heard a noise on the path from town. She shaded her eyes, blocking the glare from the lantern, and peered into the darkness. It was not a cadenced sound she heard but a sporadic noise of grunts and mumbles. She thought it might be one of the boars that ran wild in the jungle. Over the years pigs had run off and mated, and a sizable number lived in the thick undergrowth. Sometimes, they foraged in the town's garbage pile. Once, Lupe remembered, a boar had entered the village and dragged a child into the jungle before townspeople had frightened it away. The child lived but carried the scars to this day. Lupe knew; he was a customer.

Sanchez lurched into sight, his shirt unbuttoned and shoes swinging back and forth from his neck. His shirt was wet with sweat and his black hair hung down over his forehead. He sighted the woman sitting by the lantern and halted.

"Are you the whore, Lupe?"

Lupe looked at Sanchez who had thrown his shoes to the ground. He weaved slightly. He was still beyond the lantern's range and she could not see his face.

"Yes. What do you want?"

He came toward her, his feet slapping the ground deliberately. "What does a man usually want with a whore?"

Standing before her, he reached out and lifted the lantern. "Let's see what this whore looks like," he said. He peered at her intently, lifting and lowering the lantern so that he had an overall view. Satisfied, he grunted and sat the lantern down and took a seat beside her.

"You're a fine-looking whore. I'm surprised to find such a whore in this pisshole of a village."

Lupe took in the man who sat beside her. He was big and had been drinking. She had learned that the combination often meant trouble.

"I was born here," Lupe said.

"How much do you charge?" Sanchez asked. His tone was not brusque but direct.

"Three colones," Lupe answered.

"Three colones. You mean centavos?"

"No, colones."

"Damn, whore, where do you think you are? This is not La Liberdad. Not even San Vincente. Who ever heard of a whore in a village this size charging three colones?" the sergeant said angrily.

"That is the price. I've had no complaints," Lupe said matter of factly.

"It's too much," the sergeant protested.

"I barely make a living at that."

"It's still too much."

"Then go to La Liberdad or San Vincente," Lupe said. "But, if you are a customer of Lupe of the village of San Sebastian, you will pay three colones or your prick will stay in your pants."

Her voice had hardened. She did not bargain her price. Her only concession was sometimes to do something extra, and only then for valued customers.

"Do you know who I am?" Sanchez asked.

"No," Lupe said.

"I am Sergeant Emilio Sanchez of the Army of El Salvador. I command forty eight men and we are on special assignment here."

"Why would the army send you here?" Lupe asked in surprise. "There is nothing of value here. We are so poor even the campesinos ignore us."

"The coast," Sanchez said, settling back against the wall. "We're to keep people away from the coast. One of the brains of the general staff has the idea campesinos are smuggling guns along the coast."

Lupe laughed, genuinely amused. "You're wasting your time. There're no campesinos here. They haven't been here for a long time. They found out we had nothing to steal."

"The officer thinks otherwise. I do what I'm told."

"It's a waste of money, if the government has any left to waste," Lupe said sarcastically.

"We will see," the sergeant said. "Anyhow, we have orders to keep people away from the coast." He reached out and fondled her breasts as he spoke.

Lupe ignored his hand. "But, we fish there. We need the fish to live."

"No more," he said emphatically. "You'll have to live on something else."

"But we must," she exclaimed. "We go openly in the daylight. Your men will be able to see we are fishing, not smuggling."

He ignored her, stretching his legs out and exhaling in a long, contented sigh. He laced his fingers, cracked his knuckles and looked up at the sky. "Do you have a beer?" he asked.

"No, I don't sell beer. There is a cantina in the village," she said.

"I know about the cantina. But I am here and the cantina is there. Why don't you sell beer? Men like to drink when they screw."

"The man at the cantina has to make a living, too."

"Shit on the man at the cantina," Sanchez said angrily.

"Lupe the whore, did you hear me say that I had forty eight men in my platoon?"

"Yes."

"Well, perhaps we can work out a deal. I would let them come to visit you and in return you would let me go free." The sergeant shook his head, satisfied that he had made a fair offer. "And," he added, "ten centavos to me for every one of my men who come to you."

"The *mordita,* eh?" Lupe said scornfully.

Sanchez smiled, happy she understood. "You catch on quickly. It is not a full size bite, just a nibble. I get a share and you get a lot of customers."

Lupe sat very still. She was angered by Sanchez' proposal but she knew he was dangerous. She tried to evaluate the offer objectively. It was true that forty eight customers was a lot. Still, soldiers were unstable. They could cause a lot of trouble. She sat and thought and made up her mind. But, she did not answer him. She listened to the night sounds of insects and lizards and the noises calmed her. She closed her eyes and nodded.

"Well, Lupe the whore, what do you say?" Sanchez asked.

"No," she answered.

He sprang up so quickly he lost his balance and staggered. "What do you mean 'no', you whore bitch," he bellowed. He drew back his hand to slap her and she stood and backed off.

"I mean 'no'," she said. "You cannot control your men. When they need to come to see me they will come. If you forbid it, they will hate you and cause trouble. Perhaps, Sergeant Sanchez, you are strong enough to handle ten of them. But can you handle forty eight men?"

Sanchez stood frozen, his hand still raised to strike her. This woman did not fear him, his strength or his authority. He stared at her in the lamplight and lowered his arm. She was right.

"All right, whore, let us get to business," he said angrily.

"Of course. Three colones," Lupe said. She held out her hand. "In advance."

Sanchez dug the notes from his pocket and thrust them at her. "Whores," he growled.

SIX

They had finished the morning meal and sat around the table, each silently contemplating the news Lupe had told them. They had eaten earlier than usual and the dirt floor was not yet warm from the sun's heat. From the battery radio that Juan had bought in the States a band played romantic ballads.

"Soldiers," Emilita finally said. "Nearly all my life I've seen soldiers and not one worth a damn. Why do they want to keep us from fishing? Do they want us to starve?"

She pushed up from the table. "Shit," she said.

"Emilita," Lupe chastised her. "Remember Tomas."

"Shit," Emilita repeated bitterly. "He has heard it before. And if we aren't allowed to fish, he may have to eat it." She went to the back door and started through. Stopping, she turned. "It was better when the gringos had the land and the company ran everything, including the government. At least we had enough to eat and a little money to buy something pretty. Now it's mostly tortillas. And, when's the last time we had the money to buy anything for ourselves?" She left and they heard her in the backyard fussing at the chickens.

"It's a serious thing," Lupe said, reaching over the table to straighten Tomas's hair. "Who but God knows how it will end?"

"God?" Juan said the word as though it hurt him. "When has He ever helped us?"

"I didn't say He would help us," Lupe said. "I said only He knows how it will turn out."

"You know how it will turn out. Like everything turns out for us. Bad. Since He must know it, why did He let it happen?" Juan asked.

"I don't have answers," Lupe admitted. Silence folded around them as the sunlight worked its way across the room.

Tomas left the table and spun the dial of the radio. A blast of rock music ricocheted through the room.

From outside Emilita screamed, "Turn that damn thing off."

Tomas turned the radio down. "They can't keep us from fishing," he said. "Not if everybody sticks together."

"Guns can do a lot of things," said Juan. "You stay away from the soldiers."

"But if everybody fishes, what can they do?" Tomas asked. "They can't shoot everybody."

"You don't know, Tomas," Juan said. "Soldiers can do what they want. Everybody knows it. Nobody in the village will oppose them. You'll see."

Lupe nodded solemnly. She threw her head back and ran her fingers through her hair. "I hope it doesn't get like it was when they were fighting the campesinos here. God, it was awful."

"What do you know about awful, girl?" Emilita stood at the back door. Her voice was harsh and bitter. "Two husbands soldiers have cost me. Both good men, but they were no match for the soldiers. When you," she pointed a crooked finger at Lupe, "were not yet two I buried your father. And was left with nothing to raise you.

They accused him of being political. Political? He couldn't even read. All he'd ever done was work the groves."

She began to cry. The tears flowed down the ruts in her

face until they fell off her chin. She wiped them away on the back of her hand. "Then they shot him, right in front of me, with you in my arms. Damn all soldiers."

Emilita raised her hands above her head and her voice became shrill. "How many times did I pray to God? A hundred? A thousand? And He never answered. The only damn voice I heard was Father Donaldo asking for more for the church. I hate soldiers. All they do is cause poor people trouble so rich people can get richer."

She crossed the room and stood facing Lupe. "What will we do?" she said. "I'm too old to move. I can't leave here."

She hugged Lupe around the neck and began to cry again. Lupe buried her face in the old woman's waist and wrapped her arms around her. "We'll make out somehow," she said.

"We'll take care of you Emilita," Juan said. "Don't worry."

But he offered no reason not to.

SEVEN

Lupe and Juan lay in bed. It was raining and she had turned out the lamp early. When the weather was bad, no one ever came except the priest and he would not approach the house unless the lamp was lit.

She thought back to the first visit of Father Mario. It had been on a rainy night that he appeared, a dripping figure just beyond the lamplight.

"Lupe?"

"Yes."

"Are you alone?"

"Yes. Who is it?"

He had come into the light then, water dripping from his flat, black hat and his robe soaking from the downpour. He took a seat beside her and bent over to let the water drain from his hat. "Turn out the lamps, Lupe," he said quietly.

She cupped her hand over the globe and blew the flame out. She was frightened and it showed when she spoke.

"Father Mario, why are you here?"

"Because I am weak, Lupe."

She drew in her breath through her teeth. "You mean

you are here as a customer?"

"Yes," the priest said and pressed three colones in her hand.

"You know the amount?" she said in surprise.

"I hear many confessions, Lupe."

"But father, I cannot do this. You are a priest, my priest. It is a sin."

He stood up and took her by the hand. "It is my sin, Lupe, not yours. Come, it is not safe for me to stay here too long."

He satisfied his need quickly and silently, except at the end, when he was finishing, he groaned, a gritty, plaintive sound.

Rolling free, he had lain on his back, his breathing slowly subsiding until it became deep, regular. She had thought he was asleep and after awhile had reached out tentatively to wake him.

He had taken her hand to stimulate him and, when he was ready, they had joined in a wild, frantic mating that left them spent and wet with sweat.

She was half awake when she heard him preparing to leave. It did not seem proper to remind him that he owed an additional three colones. Besides, it was one of the rare occasions she physically enjoyed a customer.

For a long time Lupe lay naked where the priest had left her and thought, wide-eyed in the dark. The robe was deceiving. He had a lean, muscled body. His fingers were firm but not rough and he knew how to use them; he had been with women often.

In the morning, when she went to straighten up, she found three colones on the bedside table. Father Mario kept his account current.

One evening, as he was preparing to leave, Lupe interrupted him.

"Father, I want to ask you something."

"Yes?"

"Aren't you Italian?"

"Yes."

"Then why are you here in San Sebastian?"

"It is a long story better left untold."

"I want to know," Lupe persisted.

The priest sat down on the bed. When he spoke, it was in low, sad tones. "Years ago, after I'd become a priest, I got a young woman in my parish pregnant. I was about to be defrocked. A powerful friend in Rome intervened. I was allowed to remain in the priesthood but only on condition I serve the poor in a foreign land. I can never go back."

He sat quietly for awhile after he finished. Then his whole body began to tremble and he broke down and sobbed.

Lupe cradled him in her arms and he clung to her like a child to a mother.

He did not come often and not on any schedule that Lupe could anticipate. But many times when she sat alone in the darkness waiting for a customer, she found herself thinking of Father Mario. It disturbed her that she thought of him as a man, not a priest.

"Lupe?"

The noise startled her. "Yes?"

"Lupe, you were mumbling, you must have been dreaming."

Juan turned on his side and put his arm around her. She felt warm and he pressed against her. "Can we talk a minute?"

"Yes."

"Do you think if both of us went to see Sanchez we could talk to him about the fishing?"

She sighed and reached out to touch him. "What is there to talk about? They have said we can't do it and you and I know they can stop us."

"Perhaps it will not be for long. Maybe a month or two."

"Maybe," she said disinterestedly.

"We can make it for that long."

"I suppose so," she said.

"What do you really think?" he asked.

The rain pounded down on the thatched roof and the wind tugged at the palms. She felt alone and frightened and she knew that Juan felt the same way. Poor, dear Juan; she loved his gentleness and kindness but she knew how weak he was. He had always felt insecure. She knew that a large measure of her love for him was pity.

She pulled him close. "I think it is time that you make me feel like a woman," she said, seeking his mouth with her own.

EIGHT

The soldiers came down the dusty main street of the village driving a young man ahead of them. He was bare to the waist and welts on his back oozed blood where he had been whipped. There was blood on his head also; it had dried and his black hair was matted to the wounds. His hands were lashed behind his back so tightly his shoulders seemed pulled out of joint. He was taller than his captors and though he staggered, weaving erratically, he held his head upright.

The procession was signalled to stop by a sergeant. He rammed the butt of his rifle down on the bare feet of the prisoner, driving him to his knees. He lost his balance and pitched forward, head first into the dirt. Slowly, he righted himself and remained kneeling.

The villagers were lined along both sides of the treeless street. From the rear of the whitewashed adobe houses, a rooster crowed, a strange sound at noon. The kneeling man's lips moved. It was hard to tell whether it was a smile or a grimace.

There was no sound from the villagers. Even the

children were quiet. The sergeant took a pistol from a black holster at his waist and placed it to the ear of the kneeling man.

A woman with a small boy in her arms, broke from the crowd, screaming. "Stop it, stop it, he has done nothing."

The sergeant, angry at the interruption, spoke to a soldier. "Get the bitch out of the way."

The man grabbed the woman and roughly pushed her back into the crowd. "Keep quiet, woman," he counselled, "or you may be next."

The sergeant fired. The sound of the shot carommed off the houses and echoed up the street. The man's skull shattered and he crumpled in an awkward heap.

It was the last time Juan saw his father. He was four.

Theresa never recovered from the execution of her husband. She called it murder and screamed curses at soldiers she saw in the streets. They laughed at her, prodding her with their rifle barrels, making clicking sounds with their tongues as though they were shooting her.

Juan, terrified, clung to her skirts and cried and neighbours chided her. Suppose the soldiers did shoot -- what would happen to the boy?

The soldiers finally left. As the trucks pulled away, she stood in the street screaming curses at them. One of the soldiers laughed and fired a shot over her head. Juan ran up the street shrieking. A neighbour found him after dark, eyes closed, trembling in the brush at the edge of the village.

Theresa became more disturbed. She stopped bathing and combing her hair. She walked through the streets muttering to herself, pushing people aside, taking no notice of their remarks. She neglected Juan, staring at him with dark brown eyes that did not acknowledge his presence.

Neighbours, pitying the frightened little boy whose mother was *loco in la cabeza*, took him home with them, feeding and caring for him. Sometimes he stayed away from home for several days at a time and his mother did not seem to notice.

One Sunday the villagers were surprised to see her going to mass. She had bathed and her hair was clean and combed.

Wearing a fresh white dress, she walked quietly to church and stayed through the mass. There was much talk among the villagers; it seemed Theresa had found a way through her maze of grief.

The next day when she did not appear by noon, a neighbour went to her house. She did not respond to his calls and he went inside. She was lying on the dirt floor with both wrists slashed. She had been dead a long time for the blood had dried and the flies were at her.

Juan was lying beside her stroking her hair. It was thirty six days from the day her husband had been shot and a week before Juan's fifth birthday.

Emilita came into the room and began to sweep the floor with a broom made of sticks tied together. Puffs of dust rose and danced in the sunlight before resettling to the earth floor.

Juan watched her and a smile played briefly on his face. "Remember at the old place in La Paz when I would sprinkle the floor before you swept?" he asked.

The old woman stopped sweeping and looked at him as though she had not known he was in the room. Her face softened. "I can still see you fixing the sprinkling can," she said. "Pounding a nail through the bottom of that old coffee can with a rock." She arched, stretching her back, and swivelled her neck, bending it from side to side, finally massaging it. Beginning to sweep again, she said, "A lot of years have passed."

"A lot of years," Juan agreed. He got up from the table bench and hugged her. "Wonder what would have happened to me if you hadn't taken me in?" he asked, pulling her to him and kissing the top of her head.

She patted his arms. "I don't know, but I'm glad I did. How could I not take you in? You were so frightened. And, such a beautiful little boy." She rocked to and fro as she remembered the times years before. "I've never been sorry," she said,"not even when you got Lupe pregnant and went off to sea."

"I didn't know she was pregnant," Juan protested mildly.

"It's interesting how men never know these things," Emilita said wryly, freeing herself from Juan's arms. She stabbed the broom at a small, green lizard that ran a few feet and stopped, looking at her through myopic, unblinking eyes.

"I came back as often as I could. And brought money when I had it. What else could I do?" he said defensively.

"It's true, you brought money." She looked at him, ignoring the lizard. "But you weren't here, worrying about where the next meal was coming from, living it day-to-day."

Juan's features sagged and he pulled a chair out from the table and sat down. "Nothing ever seems to work out for me. It's just like it was twelve years ago. No money and no job."

"You haven't really tried," she chided him.

"What do you mean I haven't tried? Where's there to try?"

"There's got to be something you could do in town," Emilita said.

"Where? Tell me where." His voice rose belligerently. "You think I don't want a job? Hell, I want to work." He held up his useless hand and shook it at her. "I didn't ask for this, you know."

"I know," she said.

"No, you don't know," he yelled. "All you do is criticize. I've got some pride. I don't want to live off you and Lupe." His breath came in gulps and his chest heaved.

"Calm down," the old woman soothed him. "We'll talk it over when Lupe comes. She'll think of something. Even when she was a child, she took care of us."

"To hell with Lupe," Juan said angrily. "I don't want her taking care of me. I'm a man, I want to take care of my family myself, not have someone else do it." Tears came into his eyes and he began to pace the room, leaving dust swirls in his wake.

"You don't know what it's like knowing your life's over," he said bitterly. "Knowing all that's left is for you to sit around, useless, and wait to die." He slammed the table with the fist of his good hand. "That's all living here is, slow death."

"I'm not fussing at you, Juan," Emilita said gently. She let the broom fall to the floor and took him in her arms. "I'm sorry I said what I did. It'll work out, you'll see. Oh, Juan, in so many ways you're still my frightened little boy. Emilita will always love you."

The lizard watched, unblinking. It did not move.

NINE

Lupe stood at the edge of the soldiers' camp and looked at the tents. There were eight of them, arranged in a square with a larger one in the middle. Smoke rose lazily from a hole in the top of the big one and she knew it was where they prepared and took their meals.

The soldiers had cleared land for the camp midway between the village and the ocean. To get to their posts overlooking the shore was a matter of fifteen minutes. More important, anyone going to the beach along the regular route would pass by the camp and could be monitored.

Off to the side, clothes hung on lines strung between several trees. Lupe watched a soldier disappear into the trees across from her. When he returned several minutes later buttoning his pants, she speculated the latrine was in that direction. There was no trash in the camp area, not even fallen palm fronds. It was an uncluttered, efficient operation.

Sergeant Sanchez came out of the mess tent carrying a basin of water. He was not wearing a shirt and the muscles of his shoulders and back bunched and rippled with the movement of his arms. He placed the basin on a board nailed between two trees.

Ducking back into the tent he emerged shortly with a two-foot length of broad leather belt which he hung from a nail. From his pocket he drew a straight razor. He spit on the belt several times and began to strop the razor.

Sanchez took the sharpening seriously. He worked the razor up and down the strap in a rhythmic cadence, stopping only to test the blade against one of his thick thumbs. He turned the razor from side to side as he stropped it and it made a smacking sound against the leather. Sunlight, filtering through the palms, reflected off the polished steel blade. He looked at both sides carefully. "Bueno," he said, and clicked the blade into the handle.

Turning to go back into the tent, he glanced up and saw her. A smile crossed his face.

"Hey, Lupe the whore, you must be a mindreader," he called. At the shout a soldier appeared in the tent opening and looked at her. Sanchez exchanged a few words with him and he went back inside the tent.

"How is that?" Lupe asked.

"I was thinking of you. Come here." He was still smiling.

"What were you thinking?"

"I have counted and thirty two of my men have been to see you," he said.

"And?"

He looked at her for a moment before replying. "I think it is time to reconsider. I should get a commission on so much business."

"We've been through that," Lupe said. "The answer is no."

He did not respond immediately and she took advantage of his silence to change the subject. Walking toward him she said,"You keep your camp very neat."

"Yes," he said. The grin vanished and he was serious. "That is important. It shows discipline. When forty eight men live together discipline is important. Without it, they become relaxed, sloppy. A sloppy soldier usually winds up dead."

"You make them toe the line," she said.

"You're goddamn right," he shot back. "They do it my way or I beat their ass."

"Do you fight often?"

"No," he said, "not often. Usually it is with new men who do not know me." He smiled at her. "Once they get to know me there are no more fights."

"You teach them who is boss, eh?"

He held up his hands before her face and made them into fists. "Here are the bosses," he said.

Lupe looked at the huge fists he held six inches from her face. The fingers were broad and short. The scarred thumbs wrapped around them so tightly the flesh was pinched white. The knuckles were lumpy and the ring finger on the right hand stood out above the rest as though it was disjointed.

"Feel them," he offered.

She took one of his hands in both of hers. It was like concrete. "It's big and hard," she said.

"That's the way you like it, isn't it?" he said with a leer. He threw back his head and laughed a harsh bark and she could see gold in the teeth at the back of his broad mouth. "That's a good joke for a whore, isn't it?"

He is more animal than man, she thought. She recalled the night he had come stumbling drunk to see her. Again she sensed the wild, raw danger in him. She smiled briefly, not wanting to displease him.

"I'm going to shave now. Stay, keep me company," he invited. "Stay right there, I'm just going to get some soap," he said going into the tent. He was back in a moment with a green, plastic soap container and a six-inch metal mirror. He placed them on the shelf beside the basin.

"I like to shave," he said. "For me, it's nearly a ceremony. It relaxes me."

He bent over the basin and splashed water onto his face. The muscles in his back bulged. They fascinated Lupe and she found a strange excitement in their movement. He straightened, shaking off the excess water, and took soap from the case. He wet it thoroughly in the basin and worked up a lather in his hands. With sure, quick movements he spread it over his face. Lifting his head, thrusting his chin out, he swabbed it until his throat was covered.

"What brings you here?" he asked. He guided the razor down his cheek and flipped the lather onto the ground.

"I want to talk with you about the fishing."

"What fishing?"

"We need to fish," Lupe said. "We have always depended on fishing to live."

"Well, you'll have to learn to do something else."

Sanchez shaved his throat, starting at his left jaw and continuing without stopping until he finished below his right ear.

"There's nothing else we can do," she said.

He doused the razor in the basin until it was free of soap. "My orders are clear," he said. "Keep people off the beaches. No people on beaches, no smuggling. It's that simple." He began to shave under his nose.

"We aren't smugglers, you know that," Lupe protested.

"Guns are coming in," Sanchez said.

"Maybe so, but not here. Listen to me," Lupe said, "we have to fish. Otherwise we'll starve."

Sanchez inspected his face in the mirror. He ran his hand across his cheeks, touching the razor to places he'd missed. Satisfied, he put the razor on the shelf and noisily rinsed his face. He emptied the basin onto the ground and turned to face Lupe.

"I have my orders," he said.

"Please, Sanchez. We'll work out a deal. You can do it. You can let us fish."

He massaged his cheeks and pushed his hair back from his forehead. His dark brown eyes continued to stare at her.

"A deal, eh?"

"Yes," she said. "You go free and you get five pesos for each man." Lupe spoke slowly, emphasising each word. "You'll make a lot of money and have no expenses."

"What made you change your mind? Why a deal now?" He looked at her suspiciously.

She shrugged. "It's simple. The situation's changed. You have the upper hand now."

"But if you let the word out to my men, I wouldn't have it long would I?"

"Why would I do that?"

"I don't know. That's what bothers me."

"I give you my word I won't. I don't want to harm you. I merely want the people here to be allowed to fish. Their situation's getting critical."

Sanchez pulled at his lip. Sighing, he shook his head.

"Lupe, the whore, you tempt me, but it's no go. Suppose you told one of these bastards," he gestured at the tents, "and he squealed on me. Do you know what would happen? They'd tie me to a barrel and each man in my platoon would whip me."

From one of the tents a man laughed and said something. The remark prompted a burst of laughter from others. The sound distracted Lupe and she looked to see which tent the noise came from.

Sanchez stepped toward her and took her by the shoulders. "Have you ever seen a man after he's been whipped? You can count his ribs through the blood. There's no skin left." He shook his head. "No deal."

Lupe stepped free of him. Without another word, she turned and walked away.

"I'll visit you tonight, Lupe the whore," he called. "You'll feel how well I shaved."

The smirk on his face remained in her mind as she walked down the path home.

TEN

The boys sat behind the cantina and watched a plane pass overhead to the south. It was still light but they could see the red light under the belly of the plane blinking until it was out of sight.

"Going to Managua, I'll bet," Jorge said.

"How you know?" Guillermo said. "Maybe it's going to San Salvador."

"In that direction?" Jorge pointed to the sun. "That's west. It's going south. Besides, it's Taco. They stop in Managua."

"Stop in San Salvador, too," Guillermo said argumentatively.

"Who cares where the damn plane's going," Pepe said. "We ain't on it."

"These damn soldiers don't leave soon, we won't be seeing any more airplanes," Jorge said. "We'll all be dead."

"Been over a month now since I've had any fish," Enrique said. "I stay hungry."

"Tortillas, tortillas, I'm so damn sick of nothing but tortillas," Guillermo complained. "When do you guess the soldiers will leave?"

"My father says they'll be here awhile yet even though they haven't seen any smugglers," Pepe said.

"At least he's making money," Jorge said bitterly.

"Sometimes they don't pay," Pepe said. "Especially the sergeant."

"See his muscles?" Enrique said. "He's tough."

"He drinks a lot," Pepe said. "Screws a lot, too, so my father says."

"How about it, Tomas? Sergeant visit Lupe often?" Guillermo asked.

Tomas shrugged. "I don't know."

Talk wound down and finally stopped. They sat quietly as the sun lowered behind the trees. In the cantina a bottle broke and a man cursed. It was nearly dark when Tomas spoke again.

"The soldiers are sucking us dry. Nobody has any spirit," he said.

"You're right about that," Pepe said. "Everybody is scared."

"Why don't we all go fishing together?" Tomas asked.

"Are you crazy?" Pepe said.

"Want to get killed?" Enrique spoke in amazement.

"I mean it," Tomas said. "We going to just sit around and talk about starving? Let's do something about it. They can't kill all of us."

"Listen to the big man," Guillermo said with a sneer. "Ain't got a hair on his prick and he's going to take the soldiers on. I can hear him talking to Sergeant Sanchez right now."

The others laughed as darkness closed in. From the cantina two men began to argue about a bet. Pepe's father lit the lamps and the light seeped out the windows onto the grass. Lightning bugs blinked in the trees. There was no wind and the sky was clear.

Tomas stood up and brushed the seat of his pants. "You'll see," he said. He walked off into the night. They watched him go. Nobody yelled a taunt after him.

ELEVEN

Tomas left the house while the moon was still up. There were huge clouds. They kept the path to the beach in near darkness for minutes at a time. The wind came in spurts, smashing at the trees, and the clouds swept across the sky, towering and black.

For several weeks, Tomas had planned for tonight. He was going to fish and be home before dawn. He planned to try his luck north of where Juan and he usually fished. His plan was simple: he would wait for clouds to hide the moon and sprint across the beach in the darkness. Once he was in the water, he was not worried that he would be discovered.

He did not know the bottom well at this stretch of beach, but this did not worry him. He was a good swimmer and he didn't plan to go far out. He would fish just outside the breaking surf and float with the net. He planned to be through and on his way home by the time the moon was all the way down.

Palms fronds swayed in the wind and rasped against each other. Before he reached the soldiers' camp, he cut inland

and passed well out of sight of it. A storm was making up. Tomas smiled. If it broke while he was still in the water, the rain would help to conceal his return trip across the beach.

Several hundred yards before the steep climb to the top of the hill, Tomas took a course parallel to the ridge. It was rough underfoot and he stumbled over roots and vines. He walked quickly, one hand before him to fend off branches and bushes. In the other he grasped the net. He was counting as he went and after he had taken two hundred steps he started up the hill.

The hill was not as steep here but he couldn't go straight up. He quartered the slope, zigzagging, pulling himself up by shrubs. It was tough going and he was breathing hard when he felt the first wind off the ocean and knew he was near the top. He stopped to catch his breath and slowly mounted the last few steps to the crest.

The ocean, driven by the wind, ran in long swells that rolled in to meet the beach with a fury that sent the water cascading skyward before it fell back and spread across the sand in long, onyx arcs. Tomas ran his tongue over his lips. He tasted salt, felt its sting in his eyes. The wind was gusting, and he bent forward, leaning into it, hugging onto the net.

Farther out, the ocean rolled in huge troughs, black and angry. He had never been in the ocean when it was this rough. He could smell rain in the wind, a storm was building. He knew he must fish quickly or abandon his plan. He did not want to be in the water when the storm hit.

There was no one in sight and he left the crest and made his way down the hill. He reached the long lines of palms and moved through them quickly. When he reached the last row that bordered the beach, he dropped his pants. He held the net tightly and, when the moon was covered by clouds, sprinted across the beach and entered the water at a run.

Its chill shocked him. He stopped, waist deep. Incoming waves knocked him down, dragged him along the bottom. Regaining his footing, he shivered; part cold, part fright.

He dove through a roller and came up in chest high water. He swam out, beyond where the waves were breaking. Putting his hand through the loop, he threw the net. It sank beneath the surface. He let it float for a minute and, feeling no resistance, drew it in and threw it again. Water broke over his head, blinding him. He pushed off the bottom, floating in the troughs. The undertow tugged at him, pulling him out to sea. He swam hard, struggling back to his original position to cast the net again. It sank beneath the surface and he prayed to feel the thrashing of a trapped fish.

Far off lightning flashed, followed by the dull rumble of thunder. Tomas was getting numb, he knew he could not stay in the water much longer. He pulled the net in and threw it out. It had hardly disappeared when he felt a pull on his arm and knew he had a fish. Treading water, he pulled the net in, hugging the fish against his belly. His teeth were chattering and he knew he was through fishing, that he had to get out of the water.

He turned on his side and tried to swim with one arm. The current was too strong, he made no headway. Twisting the mouth of the net several times, he took it in his teeth. Riding down a trough he waited until a wave crested and then swam with all his might. The wave carried him toward the land at a furious pace until it broke and smashed over him, burying him in a torrent of water. He went under, hit bottom and pushed up. As he broke the surface, another wall of water smacked him back under. He rolled along the bottom until he got his feet beneath him and fought his way to the surface. The water was shallow, he could stand. He was exhausted and near to giving up when a wave hit him broadside and knocked onto shore.

He lay on his belly, vomiting on the fish. He heaved until nothing came up. Shaking with cold and exhaustion, he crawled above the waterline and collapsed.

Slowly, Tomas came to, felt the waves lapping at his legs. His eyes focused on the fish, watching its gills move in and out, sucking for air. He struggled to his feet and began to run across the beach to the cover of the gringo trees.

The wind, which had been gusting in fierce bursts, quit abruptly. Rain, which moments before had driven horizontally with such force it stung, settled into a gentle, steady shower. It was quiet, the only constant in the stillness the muffled splash of waves breaking ashore.

On the brow of the hill above the gringo trees, Private Eugenio Morales was midway in his tour of sentry duty. He had hunkered against the base of a palm seeking to escape the battering of wind and rain. The storm had come up so quickly it had caught him unprepared and he hadn't had time to put on his poncho. He had to relieve himself and decided to take advantage of the break in the storm to do so. He hated night sentry duty. He did not like the dark and was afraid of lightning.

He stood up and unbuttoned his pants. Standing sideways to the wind, he began to urinate. A brilliant burst of lightning lit up the area and he saw something that shut off his water. Something was moving on the beach.

He scrambled for his rifle and looked through the night scope. At first he saw nothing. Fixing the scope at the water's edge he began to sight it along the shore line up the beach.

As quickly as it had stopped, the wind and rain picked up again. In a matter of moments the storm was at gale force. He had trouble keeping the scope on line and the rain pelted him in the face, stinging his eyes and obscuring his vision.

Then he saw it. A figure carrying something was leaving the water-edge and running toward the palms. A smuggler; on a night like this it had to be a smuggler. He aimed the rifle and, when it was centered on the target, fired.

The figure crumpled. Private Morales fired again to be sure his shot was on target.

TWELVE

Juan awoke in the first gray light after daybreak. Rain dripped from the eaves and it was cool. He pulled the cover close about him and lay still, his eyes closed. He sensed rather than felt Lupe's body beside him. Curling against her, he sought her warmth. Off in the jungle a parrot fussed, the sound muffled, distant. Before he went back to sleep, he heard the rustling movements of the small lizards that made their home in the roof thatch.

A hand touching his shoulder startled him. He looked up at Emilita, still in the old dress she slept in. "Tomas is not here," she said. Her hair hung down, nearly touching his forehead.

Juan yawned and sat up. "What do you mean he is not here?"

"He's gone." The old woman was shaking from the early morning chill.

Juan eased himself out of bed. He put on his clothes and followed Emilita out of the bedroom, to the alcove near the rear door where Tomas slept. The cot was empty. He felt the cover of the cornshuck mattress. It was cold and damp.

"He's been gone for some time," he said. "Where the hell could he be?"

"I don't know, but it isn't like him," Emilita said. She was shivering badly now.

"Get some clothes on. I'll build a fire," Juan said. "He probably just woke up early and is out fooling around."

When she had dressed, Emilita put a pan of water on the round piece of metal that stood on bricks over the wood fire and served as a stove. "I'll just make coffee," she said.

At the mention of food, Juan knew where Tomas was. He ran out the door into the backyard and looked on the wall where the fishing net usually hung. It wasn't there. "Goddamn it," he said.

"He's gone to fish," Juan screamed. "The net is gone." He began to run along the path to the beach.

"Holy Mother of God," Emilita gasped. She crossed herself and began to cry.

Emilita watched until he was out of sight in the trees. She went back to the fire. The water was boiling. She threw in a handful of coffee beans and sat down at the table to wait for the coffee to cook. She began to say her rosary.

Juan ran without feeling the leaves that beat at him. The trail was muddy and slippery from the rain but he did not slow down. When he reached the soldiers' camp he made no effort to skirt it. Surprised soldiers laughed at the muddy figure who dashed through their camp, dodging tents and cooking fires.

He was nearly spent when he reached the hill at the base of the ridge. He pulled himself up the slick slope, gasping, struggling to keep his footing. Reaching the top, he dropped to his hands and knees. His sides heaved and he retched. He trembled from exhaustion. Struggling to his feet, he saw Sergeant Sanchez and a soldier nearby but paid them no attention.

He searched the ocean for Tomas. The sea, still rough, ran in long rolling swells. The water was dull grey except where the wind caught the troughs on the upward sweep and churned it into foam. He leaned into the wind, catching it fresh in the face, his eyes frantically moving over the ocean for sign of Tomas.

As he turned northward, Juan saw something on the beach midway the shore and the palms. At first, he thought it was trash washed ashore by the storm. His eyes moved on, then came back.

Juan knew what he saw was Tomas. He screamed, a long howl of pain, and loped along the hill toward the body.

Sergeant Sanchez grabbed him. "What are you doing here? You know it's forbidden."

Juan struggled to free himself. "It's Tomas," he said, pointing up the beach. "That is Tomas up there."

"He is dead," Sanchez said. "He was fishing. Morales shot him."

Juan slumped and nearly fell. "You shot him? He's eleven years old."

"My orders were plain, nobody allowed on the beach. There was no age limit," Sanchez said.

"You son of a bitch," Juan screamed. "You killed him. You killed my son." He swung at Sanchez.

The sergeant pushed Juan off and swung his rifle in a swift short arc. The butt caught Juan on the jaw, knocking him to the ground, unconscious.

Sanchez considered hitting Juan again. Blood began to flow from Juan's mouth and Sanchez lowered the rifle and shifted it to one hand. He turned to Morales. "When he comes to, let him get the body. It'll begin to stink soon."

THIRTEEN

The sun hung like a ripe boil, swollen and yellow. A needle thin black cloud, like a lance, passed across it but did not drain its heat.

Juan looked at the sun and could not understand what it was. He tried to sit up; the effort left him sick. He vomited and, in trying to clean his face, touched his mouth. The pain struck him like a knife thrust and he screamed.

The soldier did not move to help him as Juan forced himself to stand. "Your jaw is broken," the soldier said. Your face looks like a fried egg sliding off a plate."

Juan tried to speak. No words came. His jaw throbbed with a terrible pounding and blood dripped onto his shirt.

He remembered then: seeing Tomas's body and the blow by Sanchez. He ignored the soldier and looked up the beach. Tomas' body was still there.

He pointed to Tomas. His body seemed to shrink, as though a giant hand was compressing it. His breath came in irregular gulps. He stood, arm stretched out, unable to speak.

The soldier looked at him with disinterest. "Sergeant

Sanchez said you could get the boy," he said. Shifting his rifle, he walked off and sat down in the shade of a stunted palm.

Juan was dizzy and his eyes hurt. He fought off the pain and started down the ridge. The angle was steep and he stumbled, grabbing at plants to keep his balance. As he lurched down the hill, he moaned, a ragged whisper, deep in his throat.

At the base of the hill, he paused in the shade and leaned against a gringo tree. He was light-headed and vomited again. He knew he had to keep moving or he would collapse. He forced himself to go on.

One of the bullets had entered the right chest of Tomas and had come out through his back. The other had torn his stomach apart. His face had not been harmed. He lay on his side, his body crusted with dried blood.

Juan had never been so conscious of how slight Tomas was; or how graceful his limbs. One arm was fully extended, resting atop his hip; the other clutched the net. The fish was still in it. It had already stiffened. Flies rose in a swarm, buzzing as Juan kneeled and freed the fish. It might have weighed a pound. He threw it aside and the flies found it immediately.

Juan leaned over to pick Tomas up and his head felt so heavy he pitched forward. He crawled to the ocean's edge and scooped water up in his hands and poured it over his head. His jaw ached, pain pulsating with every beat of his heart. He splashed more water over his head and slowly began to feel steadier.

He lifted Tomas and started home. Later, he couldn't remember on which side of the hill Lupe met him. He knew she was with him because he could hear her crying. But, it was just a noise to him.

He would not allow her to help him carry Tomas. He stumbled along, feet following the path by instinct. He reached the house and placed Tomas in the bed that he and Lupe shared. Collapsing onto the floor, he did not feel it when Lupe straightened his cramping arms.

FOURTEEN

"On the ridge overlooking the ocean," Juan said. His jaws were wired and he had to mouth the words through clenched teeth.

The ride in the kerosene truck from the doctor's office in La Senita had been awful. He remembered every rut in the road coming back. The throbbing in his jaw was intense when he sat up or turned his head. He lay on his back in bed, his neck rigid. His eyes were closed.

Lupe leaned over and put a damp rag on his forehead. He looked at her and took her hand in his. He squeezed it and held it to his chest. She bent forward until her face was close. He could smell her breath. She mouthed a kiss at him. He thought she looked tired. Her eyes, swollen from crying, were dull with sadness.

"If Sanchez will let us, that's where we'll bury Tomas," she said. She spoke listlessly.

"Goddamn Sanchez". The harshness of Juan's voice frightened Lupe and she withdrew her hand and sat up straight. "I am going to bury Tomas on the ridge. To hell with what Sanchez says." The burst of emotion left Juan panting and his head pounded from the movement.

"Calm down, you'll hurt yourself." She took the rag from his head, dipped it into the basin and placed it back across his forehead.

Emilita came into the room. "There are two soldiers outside, Lupe. They're asking for you." The old woman was barefoot and wore a shapeless shift.

"What do they want?" Lupe asked.

"I don't know."

Lupe patted Juan's arm. "Be right back."

Emilita edged closer to the bed. She stared at Juan intently, head cocked to the side, lips pursed. "How do you feel?" she asked.

"Not good," Juan said.

"Your face doesn't have that sagging look since they wired it," she said.

"Good." He reached for her with his withered hand. "Help me up."

She didn't take his hand. "I don't know," she said uncertainly. "Maybe you shouldn't get up."

Juan closed his eyes in exasperation. "I'm all right. Come on."

"Wait until Lupe comes back," Emilita said, backing away.

"You said there were two soldiers. It'll take awhile," Juan said.

"What do you mean?" Emilita said.

"Why do soldiers come here. They want a whore, that's why. Now help me up."

"Not today." Emilita stared at Juan in disbelief. "They can't be wanting her today, with Tomas fresh dead and still unburied."

"They don't care," Juan said angrily. "They want a whore."

"But Lupe can't ..." Emilita sank to the side of the bed. "My God," she said. She began to cry, rocking and biting at the back of her hand. "Lupe can't. Not today."

"Lupe can't what?" Lupe had entered the room so quietly they hadn't heard her. "What is wrong? Why are you crying, Emilita?"

"I thought ... you know..." Emilita stopped talking and hugged Lupe.

"She thought you were screwing the soldiers," Juan said.

"It wasn't just me," Emilita protested.

"No," Juan agreed. "I thought you were too."

Lupe stood silently, holding Emilita. Her body sagged until she stood hip-shot, her belly thrust forward. "Not today," she said quietly. "I sent them away."

Emilita continued to cry and hugged Lupe tighter. Juan watched but made no effort to comfort them. "Help me up, Lupe. I want to see Tomas."

Emilita and Lupe had washed Tomas and dressed him in a clean shirt and pants. He lay on his cot, eyes closed, hair parted and combed. Lupe helped Juan to kneel by the bed so he could see Tomas up close. He stared at the body and reached over and touched his arm. "He never filled out."

"No," Lupe said, "he was thin. But, I think he would have been tall, like you."

"You could tell by his legs," Emilita said. "He had long legs."

"He never knew I was his father," Juan said.

"Nor me his mother." Lupe had tears in her eyes.

"Why didn't you ever tell him?" Juan asked.

"Who wants a whore for a mother? It is hard enough growing up," she answered.

"He knew we loved him, though. Don't you think he knew we loved him?" Juan said.

"Of course," Emilita broke in. "And, I think, deep inside, he knew you were his parents."

"He never showed me a sign," Juan said. He reached over again and rubbed Tomas' arm. "So little." They looked at the body a long time. A fly buzzed, the sound abnormally loud in the quiet, and Juan roused.

"We must bury him," he said. "This evening."

"Yes," Lupe said.

"I want the grave on the hill with his head facing the sea," Juan said. "Get Manuel and his son to dig the grave. Tell Manuel when I am able, I will sweep the cantina for a month to repay him. They should dig the grave now."

"We have not asked Sanchez," Lupe said.

"Sanchez said we can't go to the beach. The hill is not the beach," Juan said quietly. "The hill was Tomas' favourite place and I am going to bury him there." Lupe helped him to his feet. "I never had the money to give him much of anything," Juan said forlornly. "I can at least give him his grave where he was happiest."

Lupe nodded. "Esteban will lend us a cart to take Tomas to the hill. He said he would do anything to help us."

"How will we get him up the hill?" Emilita asked.

"We, we three, will carry him," Juan said. "It is fitting, he is ours."

"I will get the priest," Lupe said.

"How much does he charge for a service?" Emilita asked.

"No matter what it costs we need the priest," Juan said. "Tell him I will clean up around the church when I am able."

"No problem," Lupe said. "I will take care of Father Mario."

FIFTEEN

Pepe came out the back door of the cantina. The other boys were there ahead of him, quiet, sprawled in the grass. They were silent until he sat down.

"Think they've buried him yet?" Jorge asked.

"I guess," Pepe answered. "We passed them on the way back from digging the grave."

"I still can't believe it," Enrique said. "Two nights ago we were all here together."

"That damn Sanchez," Pepe said. "He's the one who caused it."

"He didn't shoot Tomas. A soldier did," Guillermo said.

"He ordered it. I hope he gets his some day," Pepe said.

"Glad it stopped raining." Jorge pulled a blade of grass loose and ran it back and forth between his front teeth.

"Me too. Feel kind of bad, us here and Tomas being buried. Don't seem right. We should have gone," Enrique said.

"Mama said they didn't want anybody," Pepe said. "I still can't believe he did it."

"Such a little guy," Jorge said. "Took a lot of guts to do

it."

"And during that storm. The waves must have been huge," Enrique said. "I wouldn't have done it."

"I think he was dumb," Guillermo said.

The other boys looked at him but didn't say anything. The sun was still far above the trees and the air was still and warm. It was too early for the evening crowd at the cantina. The only sound was bees buzzing around empty beer bottles in the trash.

"Wonder why he did it?" Jorge asked.

"Guess he was hungry," Guillermo said.

"Nah, you know it takes two to really work a net," Enrique said. "I don't think it was the fish."

"Then why?" Guillermo asked.

"I think he wanted to show he wasn't going to let the soldiers push him around. Like when he'd fight you, Guillermo. He knew he was going to get beat but he wouldn't back down."

A truck started up, then shuddered to a stop. They could hear the starter grinding, growing weaker until it finally stopped.

Jorge lay back on the grass. "Mrs. Herera told my mother Lupe was Tomas' mother."

"No kidding," Pepe said.

"Yeah, and that Juan was his father."

"The one-arm guy?" Guillermo asked.

"Yeah," Jorge said.

"I didn't know that," Pepe said. "I just figured he lived there." He lay back and looked at the sky. The sun had dropped behind the trees but it was still light. "I'm going to offer to help them with the cow," Pepe said.

"Tomas hated fooling with that cow," Jorge said. He laughed. "Remember that time we turned it loose? What's its name?"

"Angel," Pepe answered.

"Yeah, Angel. Funny name for a cow."

"Why are you going to help with the cow?" Guillermo asked.

"I don't know. I guess they could use the help," Pepe said.

Guillermo grinned. "You trying to get in with Lupe the whore?" He looked at the other boys. "What do you think of that, Pepe's thinking ahead."

"You've got a common mouth, you know that Guillermo? You always have to say something nasty," Pepe said.

Guillermo stood up. "You man enough to change it?" He moved toward Pepe.

Pepe stood up and Guillermo shoved him. They faced each other. Enrique and Jorge stood and grouped behind Pepe.

"Leave him alone, Guillermo. Unless you want to take us all on," Enrique said.

Guillermo stared at Enrique and Jorge. "To hell with you," he said. "You're lucky I got to go."

SIXTEEN

Inland, smoke from burning fields hugged the ground where campesinos were preparing the land for another crop. On the coast, a southwest wind off the sea fanned the four people who stood on the hill. They could not smell the smoke and the air was crisp, clear. There had been only one incident. Near the grave a soldier had barred Juan's way and told him,"You're lucky. If I had my way, you'd be in the grave with the boy."

Juan's eyes narrowed but he kept quiet. He looked away, past the soldier, out over the ocean. Father Mario spoke to the soldier. "Please, it is difficult enough for this man. He is burying his son."

It had been a hard journey to the grave. They had wrapped Tomas in a clean sheet and placed the body in Esteban's cart. They alternated, two pushing while one rested. In the trees along the trail, little air stirred, and their clothes were soon wet with sweat.

Juan's jaw throbbed and he had a headache. It took all of his concentration to keep going. He plodded behind the cart without saying a word. At first, Lupe had tried to get him to talk. Failing, she lapsed into silence herself and concentrated on pushing the cart.

Father Mario met them at the foot of the hill. "You have permission?" he asked Lupe.

"None is needed. We are not going to the beach," Juan said. His voice was determined and bitter.

"I don't want trouble," Father Mario said.

Juan laughed, a high-pitched rasp that rattled in his throat. "What else can happen?" he asked. "If you are afraid, go home."

"No," the priest said, "I'm here. Let's get on with this sad affair."

"You'll have to help us get Tomas up the hill," Lupe said. "If you can take his feet, Juan and I can manage his head."

Father Mario looked at Juan. "Are you sure you're up to this?" he said.

"I'll be Okay." Juan looked up the hill. "You cannot go straight up. You have to zigzag."

Lupe and Juan got on either side of Tomas' body. The priest led the way. They had to stop often for Juan to rest. When they had reached the top they were winded. Without putting Tomas down, they rested. When they recovered their breath, they lowered him into the grave, his head facing the sea.

The service was brief. Father Mario finished the mass quickly and shook hands all around. He left, holding onto his flat black hat, for the wind had picked up. When he reached the path leading down the hill, he looked back at Emilita, Lupe and Juan, looking down into the open grave. He hesitated, as though considering returning, but went on down the hill.

"I wish we could have given him a casket," Emilita said.

Juan knelt and began to push dirt into the grave. "I don't think he'd have wanted a casket, Emilita. He liked the openness up here."

Lupe got on the other side of the grave and pushed at the dirt. "Manuel and Pepe did a fine job. It is a good grave," she said. "We must remember to thank them."

When the grave was filled, they tamped it flat with their bare feet. Soon it was hard to distinguish from surrounding earth.

"I'll make him a cross," Juan said.

Lupe gathered several stones which she placed at the head of Tomas' grave. "In case it rains before you make the cross," she explained. "This way, we'll know where the grave is."

Riding a thermal, a gull glided over them, screaming.

"Let's go home," Juan said, and started down the hill.

SEVENTEEN

"Where is Juan?" Emilita asked. She sat at the table flattening tortillas. Every time she smacked them against the table, the loose skin under her chin shook. "He was gone before I got up."

"The same place as yesterday and the day before and the day before that. Tomas' grave," Lupe said.

Emilita pounded the dough, gnarled hands alternately kneading it and slapping it against the rough table top. "All day on the hill? He has got to put the boy's death behind him. It has been over a month."

Lupe sighed and slumped into a chair across from Emilita. "He can't seem to let go." She propped her elbows on the table and rested her head in the cradle formed by her hands.

The old woman wrapped the tortillas in a damp cloth and pushed them aside. She wiped her hands against her skirts, inspecting them to see that they were free of flour.

"It is one thing to grieve; I know, I have done a lot of it. But you have to let the dead go. If you don't ..." she put her fingers to her head and rotated them,"You go crazy."

"He keeps his feelings to himself." Lupe got up and stood

in the open doorway. "I don't know what to do."

Emilita pushed up from the chair. Her knees were stiff and she grimaced as she joined Lupe at the door. "Tell me, has he been with you as a man?"

Lupe shook her head. "Not since Tomas was killed."

"That is bad, Lupe. You must help him."

"I have tried. He moves my hand away and turns over."

"What does he say?" Emilita asked.

"Nothing. He doesn't talk anymore." Lupe began to cry. "I am afraid, Emilita. He is different."

The old woman put her arms around Lupe. "Let it out," she said, rocking Lupe like a child.

Juan sat on the ridge, next to Tomas' grave, looking out to sea. He had come every day, thirty seven days now, to sit in the sun and stare at the water.

At first, the soldiers on duty taunted him, prodding him with their rifles, making chattering noises, like the rapid fire of automatic weapons. But, after a week of no response, they left him alone and pulled their sentry duty in the shade.

Juan came at daybreak when the land was fresh and cool, Always, he brought a flower or a fern or a piece of green for Tomas' grave. He had developed a routine for tending to the grave. First, he removed the wilted greens from the previous day. Then, he swept the earth clear with a broom made of twigs. Last, he placed the day's remembrance at the base of a small cross.

He was proud of the cross he'd built and placed in the ground at the head of the grave. The wood had come from a packing crate that Esteban had given him.

He had cut the pieces and honed them smooth with a knife. Then, he rubbed them in the sand until all the roughness was gone and the edges were bevelled. When he was satisfied with his work, he showed it to Emilita and Lupe.

"I am going to put it at the head of his grave," Juan told them. "I want you to come with me."

Lupe put her arm through his. "Of course," she said. "I want to."

"I want to come also," Emilita said. She went into her room and returned in a moment. "Here is seventy five centavos for paint, so it will be like the crosses in the cemetery at Father Mario's church."

Juan thought about Emilita's remark now, as he removed his hat and wiped sweat from his forehead. He opened the plastic bottle he'd gotten from the trash behind the cantina and took a long drink. He poured some in his hand and rinsed his face before he put his hat back on.

"Why do you come here every day?"

Juan looked up into the hard face of Sergeant Sanchez. Without answering, Juan shrugged and turned away to look at the ocean.

"Have you gone loco? Sitting at a grave every day in the heat. What the hell kind of man are you?" Sanchez asked.

Anger began to build in Juan. The muscles in his face clenched until the tension hurt his teeth. His jaw was not completely healed and he winced. He got to his feet, glared at Sanchez, but did not speak.

The sergeant smiled. "And this cross." He took his rifle and knocked it loose from the earth so that it leaned, nearly touching the ground. "What the hell is it good for?" He hit the cross again and it toppled into the dirt.

Rage and frustration overcame Juan. He choked back a sob and ran along the ridge toward the path leading down the hill.

"Hey, you forgot your bottle," Sanchez yelled. He threw the plastic bottle at Juan. It hit him and carromed off into the weeds beside the path. Juan stopped and picked it up.

"Every baby needs a bottle," Sanchez taunted.

The mocking laugh remained in Juan's head long after he returned home.

EIGHTEEN

"I am going to kill Sanchez." It was after midnight and Lupe had just blown out the lamp and come to bed.

"Juan!"

"I'm going to, Lupe." Juan spoke softly and deliberately. "I've thought about it since the day Tomas was killed. I've got a plan."

"Juan, you can't. They'll put you in jail or kill you. I've lost Tomas. I couldn't stand to lose you, too." Lupe began to sit up.

Juan stopped her, pulled her to him. "I'm already lost, Lupe. Not to you, but to myself. I'm no longer a man. Something is wrong with me. You know it. I know it. We haven't made love since Tomas was killed."

Lupe turned on her side, hugged him and whispered, "It's just a matter of time and then it will be like it's always been. Believe me, you'll see."

"It's not just sex they've robbed us of, Lupe. It's everything. Before the soldiers came, everything was all right. Now, we are afraid. They do what they want with us and we accept it." Juan spoke quietly, no emotion in his voice. "When they killed Tomas, who said anything about it? It was murder and not a damn soul in the village complained. Not even the priest."

Lupe pulled away and sat up. "That's my fault," she said. "Who cares about the son of a whore?"

The silence built between them, heavy, divisive. The gekko moving along the rafters, rustling the roof fronds, was the only sound. Close together, they were apart.

"I care," Juan finally said. "And I'm going to do something about it." He sat up and kissed the back of her neck. "Lie down, Lupe. Let me tell you what I'm going to do."

NINETEEN

"He's got to come tonight or tomorrow. It's been over a week," Juan said. He was sitting with Emilita and Lupe in front of the house helping them shell beans. He split the pod with his teeth and stripped the beans with his good hand.

"I don't like anything about the idea,"E milita complained. "I've told you about soldiers, they're nothing but trouble. You'd better listen to me."

Lupe sat spraddle-legged, her skirt hanging like a hammock between her legs. She caught the shelled bean in her lap and threw the hulls onto a newspaper spread on the ground. "Juan feels he has to do it. I respect that. You must, too."

"What about me?" the old woman said. "What will happen to me when they catch you?"

"Nothing," Juan said. "Besides, I don't plan on being caught."

"Easy to say," Emilita snorted. "You can't fight the army by yourself." She threw a handful of hulls onto the newspaper. "Besides, what do you gain by killing Sanchez?"

"Self respect," Juan said.

"Shit," Emilita said angrily. "How much self respect will you have when you're lying in the dirt, your life's blood running out of you? Is that your self respect?"

"It'd be more than I have now," Juan said. "Sanchez plays with us. Everyone in town is scared of him. Look what he did to Tomas and he got away with it. And this," he touched his jaw. "I can't live like this."

"Lupe, talk some sense to him."

"Juan's right, Emilita. If Tomas had gotten away with fishing, it might have changed things. Maybe some others in town would have got some backbone."

"But, he didn't," Emilita said. "And now he's lying up there dead. And not yet twelve."

"He tried though," Juan said."Can't you see that?"

Emilita began to cry. "All I see is I'm old with no future."

"Stop crying," Juan said. "There are lots worse things."

"Name one," Emilita said.

"Being young with no future," Juan said.

TWENTY

"Lupe the whore, it's been a long time." Sergeant Sanchez spoke from the outer rim of the lantern glow. He held an open beer in one hand and a package in the other. The lantern was smoking and the light was uneven. Lupe reminded herself to trim the wick. "Where've you been, sergeant? It's been so long I though you'd forgotten me." Lupe's smile carried through the faint light.

"Busy," Sanchez said, entering the ring of light and taking a seat next to Lupe. "Damn officers been looking things over."

"Anything wrong?" Lupe asked.

"No, routine inspection. But after awhile it gets to you. Officers are a pain in the ass." He took a drink. "Doubt we'll be here much longer."

"You're going to leave?" Lupe asked.

"Probably within a couple of weeks." He finished the beer and threw the can away. "You'd better make the most of it."

"Where are you going?" Lupe asked.

"No word yet." Reaching into the bag, he took a beer out.

"Damn beer gets hot carrying it around. If you weren't so damn hard-headed, I wouldn't have to."

Lupe went inside the hut.

"Where the hell you going?" Sanchez asked.

"I decided to take your advice." She held out a bottle of rum to him.

Sanchez grinned. "So, you did it," he said happily. "Rum, eh?" He set the beer down. Twisting the top off the rum bottle, he took a drink. "That's more like it. Lupe, how come you changed your mind?"

"Got to thinking about what you said. Decided to make some money."

The grin left Sanchez' face. "How much you charging?"

"First one's on the house. You gave me the idea," she said.

"You should've been doing it all along," Sanchez said. He took another drink. "Way to spend an evening. Get a little drunk, a good whore. All a man needs."

Lupe nodded. "We'll see how it works."

Sanchez stood up. He staggered slightly. "What time is it?" he asked.

"I don't know," Lupe said. "Ten-thirty - eleven, I guess?"

"Think I'll spend the night. Been a long time. No more customers but Sanchez tonight. Come on, Lupe, let's get down to business."

Inside, Sanchez sat down heavily on the bed and kicked off his boots. He took a drink from the bottle and sat it on the floor. "Damn, Lupe, I'm getting drunk and I'm ready for you," he said. He pushed himself up and took of his shirt and pants. He left them where they dropped, in a heap in the dirt. He weaved back and forth, naked. "Come here," he said huskily.

Lupe placed the lamp on the table by the bed and unbuttoned her blouse. She hung it on a nail. Her breasts swayed as she moved toward Sanchez. "I want a drink first," she said.

"Good," Sanchez said. He leaned to pick up the bottle and nearly lost his balance. "We'll both get drunk." His head slanted down toward his chest and his eyes fixed on her naked breasts.

As Lupe tilted the bottle Sanchez took her breasts in his hands and massaged them, kneading the nipples until they stood out firmly. Lupe blocked most of the rum with her tongue. She backed away from Sanchez. Making a face she said, "Damn, that is hot."

Sanchez chuckled and took the bottle from her. He took a long pull of the rum, swallowing noisily. "Hot, Lupe? I'll show you what's hot." He laughed and pushed the bottle at her. Lurching to the bed, he collapsed on it, reaching for her drunkenly.

Lupe put the bottle beside the lamp. Taking off her skirt, she hung it over her blouse. She stood before him, showing him her nakedness. She propped one leg on the edge of the bed and leaned closer. "How do you like what you see, Sanchez?"

His eyes centered on the triangle of thick dark hair that she thrust out at him. "Come here," he said thickly.

Juan left the cover of the brush when Lupe came out of the hut. Her skirt twirled around her legs as she twisted her body about, searching for him. She looked as though she were dancing in the pale moonlight.

Their bare feet made no sound as they walked toward each other. "I think he's passed out," Lupe whispered. "He was snoring."

"Good," Juan said. "Wait here until I come for you."

She touched Juan's arm. "Sanchez told me they're pulling out in a couple of weeks. Why don't we just let them leave? Then, it'll be like it used to be."

Juan's face was sad. "It'll never be like it used to be. Have you forgotten Tomas so quickly?"

"Of course I haven't forgotten Tomas," Lupe said. "But killing Sanchez won't bring him back."

"No," Juan agreed, "it is too late to bring Tomas back. But maybe it's not too late to bring me back."

"They'll kill you," Lupe pleaded, "think about us."

"I am thinking about us, Lupe. It's our only chance."

He walked toward the hut, the machete shining in the

moonlight.

Inside, Juan saw Sanchez lying sprawled on his back in the bed. His powerful chest looked like a bellows as it swelled and deflated when he breathed. His mouth was open and he snored a series of animal-like grunts and snorts.

He thought of the pain the man had caused, the lives he had ruined. Anger rose in him at the memory of Tomas' small body lying on the beach. Juan screamed and swung the machete down with all his might. The blade sliced through Sanchez' throat, cutting through to the bone.

Sanchez' head lifted off the bed and his eyes opened and bulged. Blood spurted from the severed arteries and spilled onto his chest. His lips contorted as he strained. His arms jerked upward, then fell back to the mattress jerking convulsively.

Juan leaned down until inches separated their faces. "That was for Tomas, you son of a bitch," he said. Sanchez' eyes were still open and a shudder shook his body. "And this is for me," Juan said, swinging the machete into him again.

Blood covered the sergeant's upper body. Sanchez looked like a side of beef that had been butchered. He had been dead a full minute before Juan stopped hacking him with the machete.

Outside, Lupe heard the smack of the machete on Sanchez' body. She shuddered, even as it satisfied her.

TWENTY ONE

The Major stood on two boards placed across a pair of beer cases. He was a short, slight man and the make-shift platform elevated him a foot above the prisoner who stood before him. The villagers, whom he had ordered assembled, lined San Sebastian's only street. Soldiers from Sergeant Sanchez' platoon stood at intervals in front of them. The crowd was silent in the dirt road; they knew what was going to happen.

Bare-headed, still in the blood-stained clothes he was wearing when captured, Juan stood with his arms tied behind him. He was indifferent to the soldiers who flanked him.

It had taken the soldiers less than six hours to capture him after Sanchez' body was discovered. He was trying to reach La Liberdad, to stow away on a coastal freighter. They found him crossing a field on the edge of town and beat him pretty good before they brought him back.

His eyes searched the crowd for Lupe and when he saw her a smile broke over his face. "Lupe, come here," he called.

Lupe sauntered out into the street, looking at the soldiers with disgust. They moved to stop her but the Major motioned to let her alone. She had bathed and put on a clean yellow dress. Her hair was pulled straight back and tied behind her neck with a yellow band. It accentuated high cheek bones, a gift from Indian ancestors. She moved directly to Juan, put her arms around his neck and kissed him.

"You are beautiful."

"I want to look good, so you'll remember me." Her arms were still around his neck.

"Two things I remember well and happily - - you and Tomas. And Emilita, of course. Mostly you, since we were children." He looked around over the crowd. "The rest I won't miss."

"Emilita is not coming. She said to tell you goodbye, she loves you."

Juan nodded. "Thank her for me. I'm glad it's just you."

"Why didn't you try to get away?" she asked. "You didn't really try."

"No," he admitted. He shrugged. "There was nowhere to run and nothing to run for." He paused and looked down the street and then up at the sky. "I'm not afraid. This way it's over quick. I'm ready for it. The other way - dragging it out, waiting day after miserable day until you get old and die - was what scared me."

She put her head on his shoulder and he bent his head until it touched hers. "I know. I sensed it. Since Tomas' death, I've noticed a difference," she said.

"Before then, really."

The Major began to speak to the crowd, to explain why Juan was a prisoner and why he would be shot. Neither Juan nor Lupe paid him any mind.

"Will you stay in San Sebastian?" he asked.

She seemed surprised. "I don't have a choice."

"Get out, Lupe, there's nothing here."

"Maybe later, after Emilita is gone, I will move."

"I hope so."

They stood silently. The Major's voice droned on, unnoticed. "Lupe?"

"Yes."

"Bury me on the ridge."

"I will."

"Facing the sea."

"Of course."

He laughed abruptly. "You know the palms, the ones planted in rows? Tomas called them gringo trees."

"I know. From the time he was a little boy." She smiled. "We were lucky. He was a good son."

"Yes, I wish I'd had more time with him." He paused and sighed. "Still, in spite of all the sadness, I'm glad we had him."

"Oh God, yes."

The Major stopped talking. One of the soldiers took Juan by the arm. "It is time now," he said. He pulled Lupe back.

Lupe shook the soldier off. She gave Juan a last kiss and stepped away. "I love you."

He took a last look at her as the soldiers led him away through the crowd. "Me, too," he called back. "Forever."

TWENTY TWO

"Angel's broken loose," Emilita announced, coming through the back door. "She's gone."

Lupe erupted. "Juan hasn't been dead an hour and you're thinking about the damn cow. Jesus, Emilita!"

"I'm just telling you she's gone," the old woman whined.

Lupe walked away, crossing the empty cow lot, hands balled into fists. As soon as she was out of sight of the house, she dropped down in the dirt. Her stored anger released and she gave in and sobbed.

"The cow is up ahead a couple of hundred yards."

Startled, Lupe looked up to see Father Mario, standing over her, his face shaded by the black flat-brimmed hat. He squatted beside her. "Lupe, I can't perform the funeral service for Juan."

"Why not?" Lupe asked in dismay.

"The authorities won't allow it." He took off the hat, turning it in his hands. "I'm sorry."

"How can the authorities tell the church what to do? It's a simple funeral. How can they keep you from attending the dead?"

"Soldiers do what they want, you know that."

"Even with the law of God? You're a priest, you don't have to accept that?"

"The major told me directly to stay away." Father Mario found a patch of grass and eased himself to the ground. "They want to make an example ... so the people won't test the army's authority again."

"And you are going along? What kind of a priest are you?"

"A troubled one, Lupe. I can't do it. I can't attract attention to myself. The monsignor would learn of it and it would cause trouble. It could be the end of me."

"Shit," Lupe hissed. She got up and walked quickly up the path.

Father Mario followed her and found her with the cow. "Please try to understand. This little parish is all I have. I can't afford to lose it. I won't get another chance." He looked at her, a plea in his eyes.

Angel lifted her tail and loosed a full bowel's stream of near liquid stink. The foul mess splattered Lupe's bare feet. Her nostrils flared up at the odour.

"I'm sorry, Lupe. I'll come one night soon."

"No," Lupe spat the word out. "Never again."

"But, Lupe ..." the priest stretched out his hands.

Teeth bared, she faced him. "Angel's shit is sweet compared to you."

EPILOGUE

Lupe sat up. The sun was far out over the ocean now, lowering fast. The breeze had picked up, blew fresh in her face. The gringo trees bent before it, palm fronds thrashing, rasping against each other. Lupe reached out and smoothed the dirt on the grave, not an hour filled.

On the beach below, waves had cut a ditch through the sand. A pool of water had collected, trapped by the turning tide. Gulls stalked deliberately around its edges, probing for minnows.

A moan, like wind playing under a roof's eaves escaped Lupe's lips and lingered. She patted the grave again. "Goodbye," she said. She stood up, still staring at the mound. Tears started and she brushed a hand across her eyes.

Farther down the ridge, a pair of soldiers watched her get up. "Hey, Lupe," one of them called. "You going to be open for business tonight?"

Lupe stared at the soldiers. Her loosed hair swirled around her head. Mopping at her eyes with her knuckles, she thrust her shoulders back and started down the hill home.

"Why not?" she called back.